THE DILAPIDATED DETECTIVES DOWN UNDER

Paul Weinberger

Copyright © 2021 Paul Weinberger

All rights reserved

The characters and events portrayed in this book are fictitious. Any similarity to real persons, living or dead, is coincidental and not intended by the author.

No part of this book may be reproduced, or stored in a retrieval system, or transmitted in any form or by any means, electronic, mechanical, photocopying, recording, or otherwise, without express written permission of the publisher.

Cover design by: Fivespoons

CHAPTER ONE

Chief Constable Selby had convinced himself he was suffering from some sort of psychological syndrome. The evidence had been mounting up over the preceding eighteen months and was now hard to ignore. The trouble was, he found it difficult to articulate exactly what the condition was, not least because he felt wrapped up in it. His best attempt at a description – Keep Coming Back For More Even When You Know It's Painful Syndrome – didn't even sound memorable, let alone medical.

He sat in the passenger seat of Sergeant Deacon's car, being driven to the flat of Claude Simmons. And it was Claude Simmons who had very much caused this bout of self-analysis. He was formerly a Detective Chief Superintendent in the Metropolitan Police and had been the Chief Constable's mentor for the early part of his career. Now in his eighties Claude should, by all reasonable expectations, have been enjoying a well-earned retirement. But instead he had decided to make a comeback and had involved himself in a major murder inquiry. Well, three major murder inquiries.

Worse still, he had joined forces with another octogenarian, Marjorie Watson. Compulsively outspoken and with an Olympic-standard impetuosity, she was very much the yin to Claude's yang. Or, to put it more accurately, very much the Vlad The Impaler to his logical, considered problem solver. Together, they had quickly developed a novel crime detection technique which basically involved them constantly placing themselves in harm's way, much to the Chief Constable's exasperation. To his further annoyance they had even given their technique a nickname: The Pensioner's Superpower.

Claude and Marjorie's first case had involved the murder of their friend, Audrey Patterson, in the retirement home where they were all living. That was when the Chief Constable's pain began. While his own investigative team dithered, Claude and Marjorie had stepped in and solved the case in double quick time. In trademark fashion, Claude had deliberately goaded the lead suspect in the case and had narrowly escaped being murdered himself.

Never again, vowed the Chief Constable. Until six months later when he found himself inadvertently tangled up with Claude and Marjorie in a second murder inquiry. Followed some time afterwards by a third.

Yet here he was, about to climb back on the horse again. In his defence, Claude and Marjorie were extremely effective at what they did. They had solved an astonishing six murders and he wasn't above bathing in the reflected glory of their success. His Serious Crime Statistics were now the envy of every police force in the country. Also, the new case he was about to bring them would almost certainly allow him to keep some distance between himself and the chaos they might cause. Nonetheless, he had the distinct sensation of stepping out onto the spider's web again.

The Chief Constable tried to drag Sergeant Deacon into the debate, perhaps hoping for a bit of moral support. He explained the ambivalence he felt about offering the new case to Claude and Marjorie.

'It must be something to do with the fact that pain only exists in the short term memory, don't you think?' he asked, trying to sound scientific.

The Sergeant listened intently. He was convinced he already knew the name for the psychological syndrome in question but felt it was inappropriate to suggest it. Fortunately, the Chief Constable was still in full flood.

'It's a bit like that rower chap,' he continued. 'There he was, totally exhausted after winning his fourth gold medal and giving everyone permission to shoot him in the head if they saw him anywhere near a boat again. Four years later he was back in the boat, looking like death warmed up and about to collect his fifth gold medal.'

The Chief Constable also had an anecdote about his wife giving him similar instructions at the birth of each of their four children but, on balance, decided it was too detailed to share with the Sergeant.

'And then there's that Arctic explorer,' he eventually went on. 'He comes back minus a couple of toes and vows never again. The next thing you know he's trudging round the Antarctic, minus a couple of fingers.'

Sergeant Deacon was fairly convinced that several explorers had been mixed up together here, not to mention several digits.

In any event, the Chief Constable had more or less exhausted his rant. He turned to the Sergeant. 'Well, come on,' he said, reprimanding him unfairly for his silence. 'You went to a fancy university. What do you think?'

Sergeant Deacon had indeed attended a good university but had actually read computer science. Nonetheless, having been upbraided by his commanding officer, he now felt justified in offering his opinion.

'I think it sounds like good old-fashioned masochism,' he heard himself say.

The Chief Constable turned to the Sergeant, shocked. It was as if someone had just burst his party balloon, right in his face.

'Sir,' added the Sergeant, in a belated attempt to soften the blow.

Fortunately, they had arrived at Claude's flat, thus bringing the discussion to a close. They traipsed up the stairs in silence and rang the doorbell. Claude Simmons answered the door and ushered them towards the lounge. They were immediately confronted by Marjorie Watson.

'Ah, Chief Constable,' she said, beaming. 'You're a glutton for punishment, aren't you?'

The Chief Constable looked at the Sergeant. The Sergeant shrugged.

'The Chief Constable launched straight in as soon as he sat down. He was keen to reassert some authority and, in particular, make it plain he wasn't just blithely handing Claude and Marjorie one of his squad's open cases.

'The victim's name is Stephen Kenny. And it's his wife who's requested your help in solving the murder. Not least because she's the prime suspect.'

Claude and Marjorie exchanged a glance.

The Chief Constable continued. The couple were actually on their honeymoon and had been married for just four days when the murder took place. They had been walking to dinner through the gardens of the exclusive hotel where they were staying when a rifle shot rang out. In front of his wife, Stephen Kenny had crumpled to the ground, felled by a single bullet to the head. It was sudden, brutal and bloody. Death was almost certainly instantaneous.

Claude was intrigued. Marjorie already had a number of questions and was struggling to stifle an early interruption.

The murder had taken place almost a year before in Australia's Northern Territories, the Chief Constable went on. It had attracted huge attention across Australia and the hotel had been quickly mobbed by camera crews and outside broadcast vans. To this day, a small media presence remained camped outside. Given the remoteness of the location the nearest police force was to be found in a small town over eighty miles away. It comprised two officers. Unsurprisingly, they had struggled with the case and even with reinforcements and a full forensic team from Darwin, the state capital, they had failed to make any significant progress. The murder remained stubbornly unsolved.

Marjorie interrupted. 'But why is the wife the prime suspect? Presumably she wasn't carrying a rifle over her shoulder on the way to dinner?'

The Chief Constable ignored Marjorie's attempt at satire. The only thing the local police were certain about was that Mrs Kenny had not fired the gun. 'But in the absence of much other evidence, she's still the one with the motive I'm afraid,' he said. He looked across to Sergeant Deacon.

The Sergeant flipped open his notebook and found the relevant details. He had been responsible for assisting the Northern Territory Police by researching the couple's background in England. The first thing he'd found was that they'd jointly taken out an insurance policy against each other's lives when they'd married. In the event of one dying, the other received one and a half million pounds.

'And she's been paid out?' asked Marjorie, bluntly.

'No, that's the whole point. She hasn't,' the Sergeant replied. 'The insurance company's frozen the claim while the murder investigation remains open.'

Claude listened to this. He got up from his armchair and walked slowly towards the window, apparently lost in thought. He stared out for a while, trying to make everything add up. Eventually he turned back towards the others.

'Well, it's a great deal of money. Even so, you seem to be suggesting that she might have hired someone to murder her husband right in front of her, four days after she married him. And when I say murder I probably mean execute. That would make her a stone cold psychopath, wouldn't it?'

'Well, that was certainly the conclusion the Australian media jumped to. But you can be the judge of that when you meet her,' said the Chief Constable, perhaps more dismissively than he intended. Actually, he was intrigued to know what Claude would make of the murder suspect, particularly given the fact that the evidence against her was entirely circumstantial. He had trained under Claude and had tried to learn from the psychological analysis he always brought to police work. Claude had effectively pioneered the art of profiling, long before it became the vogue.

They discussed the details of the case for a while longer and the Chief Constable eventually got up, signifying the end of the briefing. He and the Sergeant made their way to the door but the Chief Constable turned back, frowning. He had one final announcement to make but, given his earlier deliberations, was finding it difficult to bring himself to say it. He cleared his throat.

'After considerable thought,' he said, eventually, 'I've decided to extend your Special Adviser status for the duration of the case.'

Claude was pleased. Special Adviser was an arrangement whereby non-police specialists could be given access to police records when they were working on a case. It was normally reserved for pathologists and forensic scientists but it had worked well for Claude and Marjorie in helping them solve the Lord Jacob Unsworth murder, their third case. The Chief Constable knew this was effectively giving an official stamp of approval to whatever chaos they might cause but, in truth, it would be impossible for them to work on the Kenny case without it.

To begin with, it meant that Claude and Marjorie could immediately have access to all of Sergeant Deacon's investigation notes. This would afford them something of a grounding in the case.

'And it will give you at least some sort of credence with the Australian police,' the Chief Constable added. 'Not sure what they'll make of you otherwise.'

And on that slightly grudging note, he turned and left.

Claude closed the front door and walked back into the lounge. He found Marjorie looking anxious. He was surprised. He expected her to be excited about a possible trip to Australia and delighted about the continuation of her Special Adviser status. Or Special Agent as she liked to call it. She had never been squeamish before. Had she found the details of this murder upsetting?

'I've packed poorly,' she said, confounding Claude's expectations immediately.

She was staring at her suitcase which stood alone in the hall. Most of the time, she lived at the Fern Lea retirement home but whenever there was a new case to solve she moved into Claude's spare room. She had packed in expectation of the Chief Constable's visit but had done so on the basis that it was early January in England. Accordingly, her suitcase bulged with heavy gauge tweed, cable stitch knitwear and stout shoes. On a hook in Claude's hall hung her pride and joy – a double breasted woollen worsted coat, normally reserved for the winter funeral season at Fern Lea.

She googled the average daily temperature in Darwin: thirty two degrees Celsius. And humid.

'My mother used to say a good thick coat can keep the summer heat out,' she reminisced, perhaps trying to salvage something from the packing debacle. 'Having said that, she might have been basing her calculations on Shropshire.'

◆ ◆ ◆

Two days later, Claude and Marjorie set off for the home of the chief suspect, Stephen Kenny's wife. The Australian police had eventually been forced to release her due to a lack of hard evidence and she had returned home to her house in Surrey. Her name, it transpired from a phone call with Sergeant Deacon, was Helen Peterson. Claude and Marjorie chatted briefly along the way about the fact that she hadn't taken her husband's surname and Marjorie tried to argue that it was in some way significant. Claude thought it was entirely commonplace. The Sergeant had also told them that this had been her second marriage. She had two children, one in sixth form and one at university.

They eventually arrived at the house and Claude parked the Polo in the street outside. They both peered through the windscreen, trying to ascertain what they could about Ms Peterson and her lifestyle. The house was modern and severely rectangular, seemingly built almost entirely from glass. The surrounding gardens were large and very well manicured. A Porsche Macan stood in the drive.

'It's like one of those houses you see on Channel Four,' said Marjorie, dryly. 'Looks okay in the daylight but at night everyone can see you in your underwear.'

Helen Peterson looked surprised when she opened the door. Of course, Chief Constable Selby had fully briefed her about Claude and Marjorie; not just about their achievements but also about their age. Nonetheless, the fact of actually finding two octogenarian detectives on her doorstep was still a jolt.

She led them through into the living area. The decor was stark and minimalist and they sat down on sofas which seemed to reflect the rectangular design motif of the house. Severely uncomfortable, Marjorie thought.

Claude was keen to get the discussion started but was wrestling with a dilemma. He and Marjorie were about to be asked to represent Helen Peterson but they had no idea yet whether she was innocent or guilty. Ordinarily, he would be cross-examining her but he was forced to begin with a softball question.

'Where did you and your husband meet?' he asked.

'Where everyone meets – at work,' she replied, batting the answer back as if it was obvious. 'We both worked for the same hedge fund. I was an analyst and he used to be a partner.'

'Used to be?' queried Claude.

'He'd resigned over a year ago. Wanted to go it alone. Start his own fund. He was on gardening leave at the time of the murder.'

Claude listened intently to Ms Peterson's clipped, matter-of-fact answers. He already had a couple of questions.

'And you weren't planning to join him in the new enterprise?'

'No, we talked about it and decided against it. To be honest, we were starting to get under each other's feet, what with the wedding and everything.'

Claude asked how the boss of the hedge fund had felt about Stephen's new venture.

'He was, how can I put it? ... disgruntled,' she said.

Marjorie was taking notes. She wrote down the word "disgruntled" and underlined it.

They moved on to discuss the murder and Helen Peterson tried to recount the story as best she could. They had just checked into the hotel, she said, and had indeed been walking to dinner through the hotel's gardens. Arm-in-arm, in fact. Strangely, she still had a vivid memory of the beautiful flowers as they walked – Bougainvillea, Morning Glory, Frangipani. But to this day, she could recall little else. She had no idea where the gunshot came from. And in the aftermath of the shooting, she had no coherent memories whatsoever. Just a slow motion jumble of noise, tangled limbs and spurting blood.

Claude thought about this for a moment.

'Did the Australian police actually charge you with murder?'

'Oh, they were never as decisive as that,' she replied, with obvious disdain. 'They simply declared me a "person of interest" in the case which basically meant they could take my passport away for two months. Extremely inconvenient when you have a job and a family.'

Claude deliberately asked a question that he already knew the answer to.

'And they were interested in you because of what? The life insurance policy?'

'Ridiculously, yes.' She made a sweeping gesture with her arm, as if indicating the extent of her estate. 'I mean, the British police provided them with a comprehensive report on my finances straight away. They clearly know I don't need the money.'

Claude stared at her. 'Why did you take out the insurance policy at all then?' he asked, pointedly.

Ms Peterson didn't seem to fully understand the question. She shrugged. Perhaps she thought it was just something wealthy people did, Claude wondered. Or perhaps she wasn't being straightforward.

Marjorie felt it was high time she chimed in. She looked up from her notebook, intrigued by the direction the conversation was taking.

'Can I ask?' she said. 'Before you were married, did you and your husband have a Pre-Up?'

'I beg your pardon?'

Claude intervened. 'I'm sorry, I think Marjorie probably means a Pre-Nup.'

Ms Peterson was only flustered for a moment, quickly reassuming her cool facade. No, they had not signed a Pre-Nup, she said. They both had children from their previous marriages and had each made provision for them in their respective wills. But she and Stephen Kenny had lived together for some years and they owned most of their property jointly – the house, a second home in Cornwall, art, cars. The list was long and she had no hesitation in reciting it. All of it would now pass to her. But for the fact that Stephen Kenny's will was also frozen.

This brought her to the murder investigation. She was very keen that Claude and Marjorie should take on the case, she said. She wanted to have her name cleared. Furthermore, she wanted all of the legal problems dealt with. She was insistent that the life insurance company had a contractual obligation it shouldn't be allowed to renege on. She also wanted the will unfrozen.

'How much do you charge?' she asked, bluntly.

'Actually, we always work pro bono,' Marjorie replied, trying to take the moral high ground. 'It's our unique selling proposition.' She had picked up this latter phrase from somewhere and felt it made her sound entrepreneurial. She used it, blissfully untroubled by the fact that you can't really have a selling proposition if you're giving everything away for free.

In any event, Ms Peterson rode roughshod over Marjorie's attempted niceties. She seemed only able to see the world as a financial equation.

'Well, assuming you're going to have to travel to Australia I will cover all of your expenses, of course,' she said. 'And I'm happy to offer a bonus if you can solve the case. Shall we say ten thousand pounds?'

CHAPTER TWO

Claude and Marjorie drove to Heathrow. It had been almost a week since they'd visited Helen Peterson and they were still discussing what they'd learned from the meeting. As ever, Marjorie had formed a particularly strong opinion.

'So, poor old Stephen Kenny's had his brains blown out,' she said, a little too colourfully for Claude's taste, 'and she's more worried about her reputation and her insurance policy. Did you notice she didn't shed a single tear when she was trying to describe the murder?'

Claude had indeed noticed. But did a lack of empathy and social grace make her a murderer? He had dealt with a considerable number of psychopaths in his time and had, on occasion, been duped by them. The only thing he knew for certain was that they had an innate ability to conceal their true personality. At this moment in time he had no idea what to make of Helen Peterson.

They made their way to Terminal Three and boarded the Qantas A380. Marjorie, in charge of expenses, had secured them seats in business class.

'I'm only taking her at her word,' she remarked as they entered the cabin. 'She says she clearly doesn't need the money.'

It was going to be an extremely long flight, with a brief stop in Singapore, and they had decided to break up the overall journey with a night in Sydney. Marjorie had booked them into a boutique hotel at The Rocks, near the Harbour Bridge and overlooking the Opera House. Their ultimate flight would take them to Alice Springs.

Marjorie had only ever taken one long haul flight before, to Delhi with her husband, to celebrate their pearl wedding anniversary. In those days, business class meant a slightly wider seat and a bit more legroom. Now she had a seat that made into a flat bed. She was fascinated by it and began to fiddle with the numerous buttons that controlled the seat's movements. She succeeded in jamming the mechanism long before the pilot had even turned on the engines. This left her stranded at an awkward angle of forty degrees. Claude watched from the adjacent seat, thinking that it was, indeed, going to be a long flight. He pressed the call button.

A young steward arrived. He was blond, tanned and looked as if he'd been rather stuffed into his white shirt and navy blue suit. He spotted the problem with Marjorie's seat immediately and stepped forward to correct it.

'I think it's faulty,' she said, trying to offset whatever blame there might be.

The steward seemed entirely unconcerned. 'Ah no, she'll be right,' he said in broad Australian. He pressed the controls and she felt the seat move backwards, upwards and then tilt forwards. It was quite exhilarating.

'I'll come back and see you after take-off and show you how to work it all.' The steward smiled warmly.

Marjorie looked pleased. 'That's very kind, umm . . . Kyle,' she responded, reading his name tag. 'And I'll have a gin and tonic when you're ready, thank you.'

Claude shook his head.

The plane took off and they both settled down to read for a while. There was a dividing screen between their two seats which could be raised for privacy and lowered for conversation. Claude had raised it, to allow him to concentrate on his book.

Kyle brought Marjorie her gin and tonic. She started to read the first of the two books she'd bought from the bookshop at Heathrow: The Lonely Planet Guide To Australia. She was immediately captivated by the straightforwardness of Australian life and by the genuineness of Australians. She lowered the dividing screen.

'I think Australia may be my spiritual home,' she said.

Claude put down his book, wearily. 'Why?' he asked.

'Well, it's absolutely made for me, isn't it? Plain speaking. No-nonsense. There isn't even a whiff of bullshit.'

Several other passengers looked up from their TV screens.

'Look at this,' she said, pointing at her book. 'There's actually a group of funny shaped rocks in South Australia called The Remarkables. You can just hear the two people who discovered it trying to work out a name. "What shall we call these remarkable rocks?" says the first one. And the second one says, "Oh, I think you've done it there mate: The Remarkables".'

She chuckled at her observation. Unfortunately for Claude, she hadn't finished. She turned to another page in her book.

'And then there's a mountain range in New South Wales called the Snowy Mountains. You can just hear the two people who discovered it saying "Look at those snowy mountains, mate, what shall we..."'

Claude reached over and raised the screen back up.

Undaunted, Marjorie picked up her second book:

A Rough Guide To Australian Slang. She thumbed through the pages enthusiastically, searching for the most outrageous phrases. She lowered the screen.

'This is marvellous,' she said, holding up the book. 'Talk about speaking your mind.'

She decided to try out an example on an unsuspecting Claude.

'Come on then, what's the correct Australian phrase for something that's staring you in the face?'

'No idea,' he said.

' "Plain as the balls on a dog",' she answered, triumphantly. Three or four more passengers looked up from their screens.

She turned the page. 'Here's my personal favourite,' she said. ' "I'm so hungry I could eat the crutch out of a low flying duck".'

Kyle happened to be walking past at this point and appeared to take the remark at face value. 'We'll be serving dinner in an hour, Mrs Watson,' he said. 'I believe there's a very nice John Dory fish.'

Claude raised the screen back up.

Marjorie sat fidgeting in her seat for a while. Perhaps she was being unfair to Claude. She lowered the screen.

'I'm sorry Claude, very rude of me,' she said. 'Tell me about the book you're reading.'

Claude looked up, surprised. Actually, he was reading about one of his heroes, the Australian cricketer Don Bradman. He was more than happy to recount some of the tale to Marjorie.

'Imagine the scene,' he said, warming to his task. 'Headingley, 1930 and twenty one year old Bradman goes in to bat for Australia at number three. By lunch he'd scored a hundred, by tea a second hundred and by close of play he was three hundred and . . . .'

Marjorie raised the screen back up.

The novelty of the flight soon wore off. They disembarked for a while at Singapore, bleary eyed and leaning heavily on their walking sticks. They had been thoughtfully reminded by Kyle about the perils of long haul flights and deep vein thrombosis and set off to walk a couple of laps around the airport.

'I'm not sure whether I'm fighting off a DVT or building up a thirst for a G&T,' said Marjorie, struggling on and trying to sound stoic.

They re-boarded the plane with a grim eleven hours ahead of them. They decided to try and sleep and, with a little help from Kyle, managed to make up their beds. They settled in.

Claude was wide awake again after five hours. He

got up and walked to the galley to request a cup of tea. He stood drinking it and chatting to the cabin crew for a while. Eventually, he returned to his bed and lay back down, thinking about the murder case. He and Marjorie had had an extensive debrief with Sergeant Deacon before flying off. The Sergeant had been very thorough but, unfortunately, none of the information he gave them really moved the case forward. Neither Stephen Kenny or Helen Peterson had been to Australia before their honeymoon and they seemed to have no other connections to the country, whether family, friends or financial. Whilst the conjecture remained that Ms Peterson might have hired a professional to kill her husband, the Sergeant had been unable to find any outgoing payments from her various bank accounts that would point to such an arrangement.

Of course, there were others who could also be considered to have had a motive. The hedge fund CEO, James Garland, for example. As they had previously heard, he was disgruntled at Stephen Kenny's departure and may have been concerned about clients being poached in the future. Then there was Kenny's ex-wife and Peterson's ex-husband. Did either of them harbour a grievance? Or the children of the respective marriages. Was one of them resentful about a diminished inheritance?

Claude weighed things up, unimpressed. It wasn't Sergeant Deacon's fault, but he thought the list of additional suspects was pathetic. Not one of them had been in Australia at the time of the shooting which meant that they, like Helen Peterson, would have had to have conscripted someone else, someone like a contract killer, to have carried out the murder. Was that actually likely?

Back in the day when he was a Chief Superintendent in the Met, contract killings were not uncommon. If you knew the right person in the East End of London and you had the right amount of money, it was always possible. Doubtless if you lived somewhere like Chicago or Palermo then it might be possible as well, he thought. But this was Australia. In 2019. Did such a person even exist?

None of this was helping Claude's mood. Admittedly, he and Marjorie hadn't visited the scene of the crime yet or talked to the local police, but the shooting was starting to look increasingly random. And all of his training and all of his instincts told him one simple thing: when it comes to a murder investigation, there is no such thing as random.

His reverie was interrupted by an announcement from the Captain. He hoped everyone had had a pleasant flight, he said. And he was pleased to announce that they had just broken land over Australia. The cabin lights were switched back on.

Marjorie woke up. She returned her seat to the upright position and got her hand luggage down from the overhead locker. She sat with it on her lap and waited anxiously for the landing. Four hours later, the plane arrived in Sydney.

They took a taxi to their hotel and checked in. The hotel itself was beautifully situated and very well appointed. Marjorie had excelled herself. But unfortunately, they had both inherited a slight difficulty from the flight. Whenever they sat down, they immediately fell asleep. They knew they needed to stay awake until at least the evening to try and beat the jet lag, but it was a serious struggle for two octogenarians. They each went to their respective rooms to try and freshen up and change into some more suitable clothes.

Marjorie unzipped her suitcase. Before the flight, she had gone back to Fern Lea, discarding her winter clothes and sorting through her summer wardrobe. After that, she had sorted through everyone else's summer wardrobe. She had press ganged Margaret, Violet and Doris into lending summer frocks, blouses, skirts and shorts. Keen to contribute to the new murder investigation, Arthur had donated a rather battered looking Panama hat.

Now, she sat on the hotel bed for a moment, trying to decide between khaki shorts and an olive skirt. Fifteen minutes later she was woken by the phone ringing. It was Claude, waiting patiently for her in reception.

They went out for a walk around the local shops and found a branch of R M Williams. Marjorie, keen to augment her wardrobe with some authentic Aussie gear, selected a blouse and took it to the changing cubicle. Ten minutes later, Claude had to send in a member of staff to wake her. She emerged rubbing her eyes. She felt as if someone had put her body clock through a mangle, she said.

They tried to kill some time by pottering around the harbour for a while, gazing at the Opera House in the bright sunshine and watching the ferries zig-zagging across the bay. Eventually they returned to the hotel for an early dinner. The hotel's restaurant had an impressive menu and Claude ordered the chef's speciality, the curried blue eyed cod. By the time it arrived he was fast asleep at the table.

'Well, perhaps it actually was random,' said Marjorie, looking across at Claude. 'Perhaps you're wrong for once.'

They were being driven along in a Toyota Land Cruiser. Claude had been trying to explain to Marjorie his concerns about the direction the murder investigation was taking. She had no new information to bring to the debate but was pleased to plunge in with an opinion nonetheless.

'Why don't we have a wager? Spice things up a bit?' she went on, confidently. 'I'm happy to bet that the murder was random.'

Claude thought about this. 'Very well, and I'm happy to bet there will be a perfectly logical explanation,' he said. He offered his hand and they shook on it. 'One Australian dollar.'

They returned to gazing out of the window at the scenery rushing past. The Land Cruiser was being driven by Cameron, a chauffeur from the hotel where the murder had taken place. He had met them at the airport in Alice Springs. They had had a three hour flight and now they had almost four hours' drive ahead of them. The sheer scale of Australia was beginning to dawn on them.

Having said that, they were starting to feel a bit more rested. They had slept quite well during their night in Sydney and being whisked along in the air-conditioned comfort of the Land Cruiser felt extremely agreeable. They had left Alice Springs behind and were travelling through the seemingly endless red desert. It was a vast landscape, dissected by the empty road and occasionally interrupted by dramatic outcrops of red sandstone. Marjorie found it completely mesmerising. She tried to articulate her continuing enthusiasm for Australia to Claude.

He listened with interest. 'Perhaps you should think about moving here,' he said. 'You know, swap Fern Lea for Eucalyptus Grove or something.' This sounded a little as if he was trying to get rid of her which, of course, he wasn't. But he was happy to leave the notion hanging there for a moment.

She continued on regardless. 'Actually, I do have family here. My sister Bertha's son moved to Brisbane about twenty years ago. He was always my favourite, probably because he was the black sheep of the family. You know, bit of a rebel, in trouble quite a lot. Bertha's given me his number and asked if I might try and see him while I'm here.'

She leant forward to speak to Cameron. 'How far is it from here to Brisbane?' she asked.

Cameron thought about this for a second. 'About fifteen hundred miles,' he said.

Claude whistled in disbelief. That was about the same distance as London to Moscow.

Marjorie was undaunted. She appeared to ponder on

this for a second, possibly developing a plan.

'Well, perhaps...'

She was interrupted by a road train which thundered down the road in the opposite direction. It had not one but three trailers and created so much turbulence it made the Land Cruiser shudder. Marjorie's sentence was never finished.

It was Claude's turn to ask Cameron a question. He was keen to find out some background about the case.

'How's the hotel been faring since the shooting?'

Cameron looked in his rear view mirror for a moment.

'Ah, you're murder tourists then? That explains it. I was trying to work you both out.'

'Bloody cheek,' said Marjorie, bristling. She was fond of Australian directness, except where it applied to her. 'I'll have you know we're detectives.'

Cameron looked in the rear view mirror again, laughing.

'Yeah, right,' he said.

Claude and Marjorie stared back at him, stony faced.

'Really?' he asked.

'Really,' said Marjorie.

'Well, we do get the odd murder tourist,' he said, trying desperately to justify his blunder. 'One couple actually asked if they could re-create the crime scene.'

Claude and Marjorie continued to stare back, unimpressed.

Cameron turned off the main road onto a smaller track. He tried to redeem himself by returning to Claude's original question.

'Generally, I suppose things are a tad quiet,' he said. 'Well, if I'm honest we're not even half full. Feels like the murder's put a bit of a curse on the place.'

They passed a sign for the hotel. It was actually called The Farm, because, as Marjorie was quick to point out to Claude, it had once been a farm. It comprised about twelve hundred acres and was situated on the fringes of Watarrka National Park, quite close to the magnificent Kings Canyon and about three hours drive from Uluru.

If they were in America, The Farm would have been called a Dude Ranch. The most popular activity was horse riding and the hotel retained a small amount of livestock which the guests could help to herd and drive if they so desired. Guides could be provided for rock climbing and trekking at the canyon. Trackers were available to show off the local rock wallabies, dingoes, crested bellbirds and, if you were feeling particularly adventurous, assorted pythons.

Failing that, you could simply head off on your own on one of the hotel's bikes, 4x4s or camels. If you felt the need of your own private helicopter then, of course, The Farm could arrange it.

A year ago, it would have been just the place for an exclusive honeymoon.

CHAPTER THREE

The hotel billed itself as "rustic chic". The main building, which housed reception, meeting rooms, a bar and a restaurant, had been converted from the original farmhouse. There were huge old floorboards, rough stone walls and gnarled roof beams. Animal hides were draped around, interspersed with Aboriginal art and the odd strategically placed saddle. In the background, the air conditioning system hummed discretely, maintaining the rooms at a perfect twenty two degrees Celsius. Outside, there were Jacuzzis and hot tubs. A large infinity pool glistened in the sun, permanently heated to an indulgent twenty eight degrees.

Claude and Marjorie checked in and were shown to their rooms. Actually, they were given side-by-side cabins, designed to follow the rustic signature of the hotel and situated in the extensive gardens. Marjorie's cabin appeared to be loosely based on a sheep shearer's hut, but with mini-bar, tea and coffee making facilities and a widescreen TV. They each unpacked, selected a change of clothing and regrouped in the restaurant for dinner.

'Bit bloody pretentious, isn't it?' said Marjorie.

Claude looked around, reserving judgement. He spied a waiter weaving his way towards them with two menus. The waiter sported several tattoos, extremely skinny jeans and a rather angular beard.

'I'm Scott and I'll be your waiter this evening,' he said, handing them each a menu. 'Just to let you know, the special tonight is a lightly seared Mahi Mahi with a drizzle of olive oil and basil, and an infusion of ginger and garlic.'

'Told you,' said Marjorie.

He hovered by the table, waiting for them to choose. Claude settled for a ten ounce sirloin steak, apparently from The Farm's own herd. Marjorie took a moment longer, peering at the menu through her reading glasses.

'And I'll have the crocodile steak, please,' she said. 'I'm getting my retaliation in first.' She looked at Scott, grinning at her attempted joke and hoping for a reaction. He stared blankly at his notebook as he wrote down her choice. He took their drinks order and left.

They settled down to discuss the case. Marjorie was keen to know where they were going to start. To be honest, so was Claude. The drinks arrived and he sat sipping his red wine for a moment.

'I suppose the first thing we should do tomorrow is phone the local police station,' he said, eventually. 'I'm hoping Sergeant Deacon may have told them to expect us.' He was keen to hear the full forensic report and, in particular, what ballistics had said about the rifle.

'Then we should probably make ourselves known to the hotel manager. I'd like to see the guest list at the time of the murder but...'

He was interrupted by the arrival of the food. Scott again insisted on offering them a lengthy description of the ingredients and cooking styles of each of the dishes they had ordered. Claude's thread was lost.

'What about the post mortem?' asked Marjorie, slicing into her crocodile steak.

'I'm assuming the police will have a copy.'

Marjorie knew that Claude was never happier than when reading a detailed autopsy report. They reminisced for a while about their third case, the Lord Jacob Unsworth murder. They had managed to obtain a copy of the autopsy report then and Claude had quickly determined that, given the dismemberment of the body, it was likely a serial killing.

'Let's never forget the lesson of the missing testicles,' said Marjorie, slightly too loudly.

At that moment, Scott returned to clear away their

plates. He looked at their empty glasses and seemed to frown slightly.

'Are you comfortable with your alcohol levels?' he asked.

Taken aback, Marjorie looked at Scott and then at Claude.

'Is he accusing us of being pissed?' she asked.

'Well no, umm, I meant . . .' stammered Scott, his aloof demeanour starting to evaporate.

Claude sized him up. He was shifting his weight from leg to leg, anxiously.

'Believe it or not, I think he's being overly polite,' said Claude, trying to unravel the misunderstanding. 'I think it's actually his five star hotel way of asking us if we want another drink.'

Marjorie fixed Scott with a steely gaze. 'Speak your mind Scott, you're an Australian for heaven's sake. And while you're at it, we'll have a gin and tonic and a large glass of cabernet sauvignon. Thank you.'

◆ ◆ ◆

They finished breakfast the next morning and returned to Marjorie's cabin. She dialled the number that Sergeant Deacon had given them for the local police station. She put the phone on speaker.

'I'd like to speak to Sergeant Mackenzie please,' she

said, in her sunniest voice.

'Who wants him?' came the gruff reply.

'My name is Marjorie Watson. I'm calling with regard to the murder at The Farm hotel.'

There was a pause.

'You're speaking to him.'

Marjorie's one-size-fits-all view of Australians was in danger of crumbling. She had already had to deal with Scott, the hipster waiter. Now she was confronted by someone who wasn't just blunt but was obviously a world-class curmudgeon. She persevered.

'My colleague and I are investigating the murder and wondered when you might be able to visit the hotel to brief us, please?'

Another pause.

'It's already been investigated.'

'Not to the satisfaction of the victim's wife,' Marjorie snapped back.

Claude looked anxious.

'Look, we're not just round the corner I'm afraid,' the Sergeant continued, laconically. 'We're nearly three hours drive away and we have a lot of territory to look after. We can probably be over your way sometime next week.'

Marjorie shook her head, crossly. Claude leant towards the phone, forced to intervene. He had known the case was going to be difficult but the reality of being nearly ten thousand miles from home was rapidly dawning on him. They were now dealing with a police force who had never met them and over whom they held none of their usual influence. He weighed things up. Normally, he was the last person to brag about rank or achievement but in this case he was going to have to make an exception.

'Good morning, Sergeant. I'm Claude Simmons. I used to be a Chief Superintendent in the Metropolitan Police in London.'

You could almost hear the Sergeant sitting up straight in his chair.

'Good morning Chief Superintendent,' came the immediate response.

Claude explained that he and Marjorie had been commissioned by Helen Peterson to try and find her husband's killer. He also explained that they had been given Special Adviser status by the Chief Constable of their local police force.

'You know, the UK police force that went out of their way to help you with your investigation.'

This produced a lengthy pause.

'Look, now I come to think about it, perhaps I did get an email about this,' said the Sergeant, rowing backwards. 'It'll be difficult to move my diary around but . . . I'll see if I can get there tomorrow.'

They ended the call.

In truth, Sergeant Mackenzie didn't have a diary and, even if he did, it wouldn't have been very full. He was grumpy because he used to have a quiet life, dealing with missing livestock, occasional drunk drivers and a few entertaining pub brawls. The murder had taken all of that away and he very much wanted it back.

Claude and Marjorie left the cabin. They ordered a coffee from the bar and then dawdled their way to lunch with a walk around the beautiful gardens. There were probably about three acres in all, planted with a rich variety of desert cacti and tropical flowers, some of them beautifully scented. There were also a number of specimen trees, including various types of eucalyptus, ironbarks, gums and a host of palms.

'It's a bit like Kew Gardens,' said Marjorie, perspiring slightly. 'But without the need for greenhouses.'

They eventually made their way inside.

The restaurant was empty and they were greeted by a slightly anxious looking Scott. He showed them to a corner table and gave them each a menu. He cleared his throat nervously before announcing the day's special, possibly fearing Marjorie's reaction.

'The chef has created for you today a breast of organic, grain fed chicken with a girolles mushroom jus, a white truffle gel and a julienne of kitchen garden vegetables.'

Marjorie didn't disappoint.

'The trouble is Scott, we just can't keep up with the gastronomic pace you're setting. Apart from anything else, we haven't packed enough Rennies. Be a lamb and see if the kitchen would make us a nice cheese and tomato sandwich, would you?'

He looked at Claude, hoping for some moral support. Claude shrugged his shoulders in agreement with Marjorie. Scott wandered off to risk the wrath of the chef. Ten minutes later he returned with two rounds of open sandwiches: unpasteurised cheese on sourdough bread, with a ramekin of tomato and salsa chutney and a salad of garden leaves. Claude and Marjorie admitted defeat and tucked in.

After lunch, they tracked down the hotel manager and introduced themselves. This didn't go terribly well either. His name was Oliver Beckett and he distinguished himself from the rest of The Farm's staff with a well-pressed cotton suit. He had only been in the job for six months but he already wore a perpetual frown.

Marjorie had given no reason for their visit when she had booked their rooms and he seemed horrified when he learned their real purpose. The hotel was still struggling after the murder, he said, and the media were reluctant to let the story drop. It would be a disaster for The Farm if the whole thing was stirred up again. They were seated on cowhide sofas in the bar and he gestured with a sweep of his arm towards the complete absence of other guests.

Marjorie looked at Claude. There was always an outside chance that the manager could ask them to leave. For the second time that day Claude was going to have to make a forceful intervention, this time with some hard facts.

'Mr Beckett, your problem exists precisely because the murder remains unsolved,' he said. 'If this is still seen as a random killing then why would anyone stay here? As far as the guests are concerned the killer could simply return at any time and use them as target practise, couldn't he? I'm afraid you're not exactly sending out the best advertising message.'

Unfortunately for Mr Beckett, Marjorie decided to chime in as well, having done some online research earlier that morning.

'You know that social media's given you a new nickname, don't you?' she said. 'You're not The Farm anymore, you're now The Rifle Range. Free shots in the bar every evening, apparently.'

The manager did know and he really didn't need to

be reminded of it. Claude eventually broke the awkward silence that ensued.

'Do you think it might be possible for us to see a list of the hotel's guests at the time of the murder, please?' he asked, knowing he was pushing his luck.

'Definitely not. Even if I wanted to help, and I'm not sure I do, I'm afraid there are things called data protection laws these days.'

Claude had feared as much.

'But the police have the list presumably?' he persisted.

'Of course. But then they're the police aren't they?'

◆ ◆ ◆

Sergeant Mackenzie's mood had not been improved by three hours of hot and dusty driving. Much of the journey was on unmade roads and it was exhausting and uncomfortable. He turned off the final track and drove in through The Farm's gates.

As he did so, he passed a caravanette, parked on the verge and covered in quite a lot of the red desert. Inside sat a startled journalist. She had drawn the short straw at the newspaper she worked for, the Alice Advertiser, and had been keeping lone watch at the crime scene. For months she had played Sudoku, filled in crosswords, wrestled with jigsaw puzzles and generally twiddled her thumbs. Now, unannounced, a police car had arrived. She reached behind her and found her camera.

Claude and Marjorie were waiting for Sergeant Mackenzie outside the hotel's reception. It wasn't clear what Sergeant Deacon's introductory email had told him but, in common with most people, he seemed shocked to be confronted by two octogenarian detectives.

'Geez,' he said, 'I wasn't expecting a couple of . . .' He checked himself, briefly.

'A couple of what?' asked Marjorie, still convincing herself she was a fan of Aussie straight talking.

'Well, a couple of crusties.'

'And a good morning to you too, Sergeant,' said Marjorie, wounded.

Claude knew they'd get nowhere if war broke out. He shepherded Marjorie and the Sergeant hastily towards the gardens.

Oliver Beckett watched them go, standing in the reception doorway. His frown had deepened. A policeman was about to show the crime scene to two guests who claimed to be detectives and a journalist was setting up a camera tripod just outside the hotel's perimeter fence. Perfect.

'I apologise, you must have been through this a

hundred times Sergeant, but where in the garden was Stephen Kenny when the shooting occurred?' asked Claude, trying to be solicitous.

The Sergeant led them to a pink flowering gum tree that had a path running in front of it. 'Here,' he said.

'And were there any witnesses?'

'Nope. None. Plenty of people arrived after they'd heard the rifle shot but nobody saw it happen.'

'Nobody saw the gunman leave?'

'Nope.'

'And everyone's movements were accounted for?'

'Yep.'

'Even the staff?'

'Yep.'

'What about the post mortem report?'

'I can save you the trouble of reading it,' he said, dismissively. 'Bullet to the back of the head. Death instantaneous.'

That was that then. Claude paused for a moment, surveying the extensive garden.

'Presumably you've worked out where the shooter was positioned though?' he asked, deliberately deferring to the Sergeant's authority.

The Sergeant set off again, this time for the outer edge of the garden. He stopped behind a group of four ironbark trees.

'Here,' he said, gesturing with both arms to the clear line of sight back to the gum tree, now some distance away.

Claude walked slowly around the ironbark trees, trying to visualise the scene.

'And you think it was a . . . ?' he asked, attempting to prompt the Sergeant.

'A contract killer? Almost certainly.' The Sergeant was starting to enjoy the spotlight.

'Go on,' said Claude.

'Look, we found just one shell casing, so that confirms he only needed a single shot from what was eighty yards. Pretty impressive. And the shell casing was from a standard .308 calibre bullet. Used by everybody and therefore virtually untraceable. Had to be a professional.'

Claude wasn't about to contradict the Sergeant when things were going so well, but he knew the evidence could easily point to the opposite conclusion. To begin with, which self-respecting contract killer ever left a solitary shell casing behind? Certainly not one he'd ever come across. And since they seemed to have no rifle and therefore no useful ballistics, all they really knew was that it was, well, a standard bullet.

'And the shoe prints we found were from a pair of Nike trainers,' the Sergeant continued, pointing vaguely to the base of the trees. He now seemed to be more or less taking credit for all of the forensics. 'Worn by about ten thousand Australians. Deliberately untraceable we think.'

Or perhaps the killer just happened to own a standard pair of trainers, Claude thought.

'Anything else?'

The Sergeant thought about it. 'Yep,' he said. 'We reckon the killer had parked his car up by the hotel's gate, near where that journalist's camped out now. But again, standard tyre tracks you could find on any Ford or Holden. We think he was hiding in plain sight.'

Or perhaps he just owned a car that was popular with Australians. Claude continued to find the contract killer theory far too easy, far too convenient and, most of all, extremely unlikely.

They walked back slowly towards the main building.

'Thank you so much, Sergeant, that's been an enormous help,' said Claude, still in solicitous mode. Marjorie looked at him suspiciously.

'Just a couple more things if I may,' he went on. 'The Farm still owns its own livestock, doesn't it? Do they have any guns?'

'They do. Two shotguns. And both accounted for.' The Sergeant seemed pleased with his own efficiency.

'And were there any other English guests staying at the hotel at the time of the murder?'

The Sergeant thought about it. 'One or two couples I think.'

'I wonder if it's worth sending the guest list back to Sergeant Deacon in the UK if you already haven't,' said Claude, trying to sound as helpful as possible. 'He's very clever, you never know what connections he might unearth.'

The Sergeant shrugged. 'Why not?' he said.

◆ ◆ ◆

'But I don't understand, Claude,' said Marjorie. They had finished dinner and taken their drinks out onto the patio. 'Yesterday you were being tough with Sergeant Mackenzie and today he was your new best friend.'

'Check your email,' said Claude.

'What?'

'Check your email.'

She produced her phone and refreshed her inbox. An email popped up from Sergeant Deacon entitled, "The Farm guest list".

She was taken aback.

'Well, the manager refused to give us the list,' Claude explained. 'And Sergeant Mackenzie would have said it was a confidential police matter if I'd asked him for it. So, with a bit of flattery, I got him to send it to Sergeant Deacon, which he was happy to do . . .'

'. . . and then Sergeant Deacon sent it straight back to his Special Advisers,' she said, finishing off the sentence as realisation dawned.

'Exactly.'

She studied the email.

'He says he's very busy and won't be able to help for a day or so but that we should make a start with the names on google.' She frowned. 'He also says he's found something on the internet himself. Says we should google something called The Alice Advertiser. It might interest us.'

She looked at Claude and Claude shrugged. She put the search into her phone. After several seconds the Alice Advertiser's front page appeared. It had a rather tabloid headline:

"Desperate Police Hire Deadbeat Detectives"

The story was attributed to Ellie Hartmann - "our on-the-spot journo" - and carried a photo of Claude, Marjorie and Sergeant Mackenzie, taken in the garden with a long lens. Marjorie was dressed all in linen, topped off with Arthur's Panama hat.

They took the article in good spirits, not least because the police seemed to come out of it far worse than they did.

'You look like something out of a Stewart Granger movie,' said Claude, smiling. It wasn't entirely obvious whether this was a compliment or an insult.

They both looked up to find that the hotel manager had appeared at the patio's doors. He was carrying his open laptop and clearly hadn't taken the article in good spirits. He wore his deepest frown yet.

CHAPTER FOUR

Claude wasn't particularly optimistic that the guest list would produce any promising leads. It was just that it was all they had to go on for the moment and it was at least somewhere to start. They were ensconced in the bar where the wifi was excellent and Marjorie had brought her iPad with her. She opened the attachment from Sergeant Deacon's email. It was an extensive document taken straight from the hotel's register, with not just a list of names but also addresses, nationalities and even "reasons for visit".

'Two couples from the UK,' said Marjorie, poring over it. Also, eleven from Australia, three from New Zealand and one from China.

She began by googling the Australians and worked her way through to the New Zealanders. There were advertising executives, a film director, an ex-international swimmer and numerous business men and women. Unfortunately, none of them had even the vaguest link to Stephen Kenny or the hedge Fund.

Not as far as Marjorie could see, anyway. The Chinese couple turned out to both be musicians, apparently of international renown. The Farm was nothing if not exclusive.

She googled the first of the couples from the UK - the Kirkhopes from Edinburgh - whose reason for visiting The Farm was "Retirement grand tour". After some clicking and scrolling she tracked them down. She read from an online newspaper article.

'Here we are: "Professor Nicola Kirkhope honoured after thirty years of epidemiological research".'

She looked at Claude. Claude shrugged.

Marjorie moved on to the next candidate - the Cookes from Hampshire. They had visited The Farm for their twenty fifth wedding anniversary. She peered at the screen through her reading glasses. There were a lot of Cookes.

'Found it,' she said after a moment, reading from another online article. ' "Philip Cooke, Chairman of The Air Corporation. Gases for Industry and the Medical Profession".'

Claude sat up, suddenly taking an interest.

'Are they quoted on the stock market?' he asked.

Marjorie looked at him, confused. She returned to the iPad screen.

'Yes they are. Currently available at £7.42.'

'And has there ever been a run on the share price?'

She clicked and scrolled again. She wasn't entirely sure what the question meant but she found an article she thought might be relevant.

'There's this from 2017: "The Air Corporation short sold in shareholder battle". Is that it?'

'It might well be,' said Claude. Marjorie offered him the iPad and he read the article, frowning in concentration.

'But what does short selling mean anyway?' she asked.

Claude looked up from the article. 'Basically, it means hedge funds.'

Marjorie was still confused. She was not in the slightest bit financially literate, beyond knowing how to claim expenses. She had gone along with everything at Helen Peterson's house but, to be honest, had found all the talk of hedge funds and gardening leave strangely horticultural. Now she was in need of one of Claude's little master classes.

'Well I'm no expert,' he said. This was how he always began his master classes. 'But most people buy stocks and shares in the hope that the price will go up. Hedge funds usually sell shares in the hope that the price will go down.'

'Really? How does that work?'

'If they think a company's in trouble, they try and force the price further and further down. The more it falls the more they make.'

'They're predatory, you mean? Looking out for limping wildebeests?'

'You could say that. Philip Cooke's company had had some trading problems and the shares were short sold from £10 right down to £2.50. The article suggests they were quite close to liquidation.'

Marjorie was still having difficulties. This time, philosophical.

'Why is it even allowed? I mean, if you sell someone short in life you're basically being an arse, aren't you?'

'Which could well have been Philip Cooke's view of Stephen Kenny.' Claude neatly rounded off the master class.

They'd more or less reached the limits of their research and they discussed their next move. Obviously, they could contact Sergeant Deacon but he was unlikely to be able to provide a speedy response. Marjorie had the bright idea of emailing Helen Peterson. She would have all the details about the short selling of The Air Corporation. She would know the answer.

'Good to check in with her as well, let the client know we're on the case,' Marjorie said, trying to sound efficient.

They composed a quick email and sent it. Then they returned to their cabins to change and headed for dinner.

Scott showed them to their table and handed them their menus. He announced the chef's special of rare breed lamb, replete with the obligatory sauces, garnishes and, this time, emulsions. Marjorie waited politely for him to finish.

'You haven't got a kids menu have you Scott?' she asked, impolitely. 'Only I could murder fish fingers or chicken nuggets.'

'Or spaghetti Bolognese?' Claude added.

He looked dismayed. He fought back with the revelation that not only was there no kids menu but children under the age of sixteen were not even allowed in the hotel. The brand guidelines didn't allow it, apparently. Claude and Marjorie settled for the comparative simplicity of Barramundi, cooked three ways.

Their drinks eventually arrived and they sat pondering on the events of the day. Marjorie was pleased that they had finally made some progress but Claude seemed unusually subdued. He still hadn't shared with her his reservations about the whole Australian contract killer scenario.

'I know I'm normally the first to go on about motive,' he said, eventually. 'But in this case, we're all motive and no means, aren't we?'

'Sorry?' asked Marjorie, already in danger of falling behind.

'Well, there are a number of people who possibly had reason to want Stephen Kenny dead – Helen Peterson, James Garland, our Mr Cooke. But none had the means to murder him, did they?'

'The physical means, do you mean?' she asked, awkwardly.

He did.

'But I thought we were working on the premise that the killer was a professional?'

'The Australian police clearly are. I'm afraid I'm not.'

Marjorie thought about this revelation, realising it effectively holed the entire investigation below the water line. Perhaps the police knew something they didn't, she ventured.

'About the thriving market for contract killers in downtown Australia?' he responded, unable to conceal his sarcasm. 'I very much doubt it.'

'But you don't have any evidence that such a thing doesn't exist,' said Marjorie

'And I very much doubt that the police have any evidence that it does.'

◆ ◆ ◆

Claude and Marjorie returned to Marjorie's cabin after breakfast the next day. Marjorie had just spent the entire meal resisting the urge to upbraid Scott about the buffet offering only Vegemite and not Marmite. She felt quite virtuous for having held her peace. Now they were both attempting to tackle Sergeant Mackenzie on speaker phone again.

'Mackenzie,' said the grumpy voice.

'Good morning Sergeant,' said Claude. 'We were hoping to have another word with you about the Kenny case.'

Pause.

'Great.'

'Given all the crime scene evidence, I know the conclusion is that the murder was carried out professionally.'

'Yep.'

'Can I ask, did the investigation look into who that person might have been, or where they might have originated from?'

'Of course,' said the Sergeant, confidently.

'And...?'

'Look, you have to remember this was a high profile case. Darwin and Alice Springs were both involved. That would have been something they would have looked into.'

The Sergeant was starting to sound considerably less certain.

'But you have the case notes. Presumably you know what they found?' Claude persisted.

There was a longer pause.

'I'm afraid that's confidential.'

Claude gave up and they ended the call. Either the matter had not been investigated or, more likely, the combined forces of Darwin and Alice Springs had simply drawn a blank.

Claude and Marjorie set off for a walk around the gardens. It was still early and the temperature was just about bearable. They pottered along, both lost in thought.

'I take no comfort in saying this Claude,' said Marjorie eventually, sounding a little smug, 'but it's looking rather like I might win our one dollar bet.'

Claude was now in a bad mood, not least because he couldn't really disagree with Marjorie. The investigation had almost come to a complete stop. They reached the group of ironbark trees where the shooter had been positioned and he wandered around them several times more, vainly hoping for inspiration.

'Out of interest,' said Marjorie, 'how would you go about finding out if an Australian contract killer exists anyway? I mean, there's probably not a hitman-

.com is there?'

Claude's mood was not improving.

'You find someone who knows the local criminal community and you get them to ask around,' he said, curtly. 'Not hard, really.'

Marjorie ushered them in out of the sun. They settled down in the air conditioned bar and both ordered a coffee. Conversation between them remained slightly thin on the ground and Marjorie eventually got up to return to her cabin, ostensibly to read for a while.

Claude was left stewing on the case.

At dinner that night, they managed to negotiate their food order with Scott without provoking a diplomatic incident. Claude, however, remained taciturn. Out of boredom, Marjorie checked her email and found a reply had arrived from Helen Peterson. Claude moved his chair round next to Marjorie and they read it together. Perhaps this was some good news at last?

"Dear Claude and Marjorie," it began. "I'm afraid that this particular line of enquiry was extremely hopeful. Yes, The Air Corporation's share price did fall sharply in 2017. But they had made a number of bad management decisions and just announced a disastrous set of results. Almost all of the fall was caused by normal investors simply bailing out. There was some short selling, but not by our fund, I'm afraid. I am certain Stephen had nothing to do with it."

Claude and Marjorie looked at each other, dejected. Unfortunately, there was more:

"It would be remiss of me not to say that I am very disappointed if this is the only evidence you currently have. However, I will assume for the moment that you are pursuing other leads that do not require my involvement. Please remember that the case remains extremely urgent from my perspective and that our financial arrangement is based entirely on results. Helen Peterson"

Marjorie put down her phone.

'Stupid bloody woman,' she said.

Claude shrugged. Even if he didn't like Helen Peterson's abrasive tone, he had to agree that she broadly had a point.

That sat in glum silence for a while. Eventually, Marjorie had a bright idea. She saw Scott passing nearby and flagged him down.

'Scott, we'll have a gin and tonic and a glass of cabernet sauvignon, please. Large ones,' she said.

◆ ◆ ◆

They spent the next few days in something of a torpor. As ever, Marjorie was looking to Claude to take the lead in the investigation but he readily admitted to being entirely flummoxed. They decided to go back over the details of the case to see if anything had been missed. Given the paucity of the evidence, this took them about forty five minutes. They walked the crime scene again. This took them twenty minutes.

Marjorie suggested a call with Sergeant Deacon. They connected on FaceTime and he was extremely sympathetic towards their situation. However, he had no new information to impart. He had managed to study The Farm's guest list but had found nothing of significance, apart from Philip Cooke and The Air Corporation. He could find no other cross match between Stephen Kenny and any guests.

He signed off, wondering if he should update the Chief Constable on the situation.

Claude and Marjorie were starting to feel trapped inside the air conditioned comfort of the hotel. They decided on a change of scenery and opted instead for the air conditioned comfort of one of the 4x4s. They conscripted a guide and they set off on a grand tour of the property.

After about twenty minutes of gently bumping along they came to a small herd of cattle, sheltering under a pair of eucalyptus trees. Claude leant forward to speak to the guide.

'They look incredibly healthy,' he said. 'How do they even survive in these conditions?'

'Boreholes,' said the guide.

Marjorie looked at Claude. She wasn't entirely sure if this was a statement of fact or simply an outbreak of Australian slang. The answer revealed itself five miles further on in the shape of a large stainless steel pipe emerging straight out of the red soil and discharging water into a small reservoir.

'This borehole produces water all the year round,' the guide went on. 'And there's another one back near the hotel. We couldn't survive without them. Look, I'll show you.'

He drove them to the local Palmer River. It was completely dry but for a few small waterholes, teeming with birds. He steered the 4x4 down the bank and onto the dusty river bed. They drove along for a while, navigating their way around the waterholes.

'Funnily enough we're expecting monsoon rains,' the guide went on. 'The river will probably flood and burst its banks. Very dramatic for a couple of days. But for the rest of the year, this is pretty much it.'

Eventually, they set off back to the hotel. It had been a diverting few hours but they knew that the Stephen Kenny murder and the lack of evidence had not gone away. They both stared out of the window, knowing they had to return to the task.

'It's a bit like that joke about the toilet being stolen from the police station, don't you think?' said Marjorie.

'Is it?' asked Claude.

'You know, the one where the police don't have anything to go on.'

Marjorie and the guide seemed to think this was hilarious. Claude smiled bravely.

CHAPTER FIVE

Sergeant Mackenzie swung the car into the hotel's drive at some considerable speed, throwing up a cloud of red dust. Most of it settled on Ellie Hartmann's caravanette. She sat bolt upright, startled again.

Claude and Marjorie had been taking a spin round the garden before lunch, trying to build up their strength for whatever Scott's plat du jour might demand of them. Marjorie was attempting to have a conversation about the murder case but Claude seemed subdued and lost in his own thoughts. Marjorie wondered to herself whether he was quite close to giving up. She, by contrast, seemed remarkably positive and appeared to share none of his concerns. She went as far as to give her walking stick a twirl.

Their stilted conversation was brought to a close by the arrival of the manager. He was followed by Sergeant Mackenzie. They were both frowning.

'There's been a development. Would you please follow us?' the Sergeant said, curtly.

Claude and Marjorie looked at each other. A development, thought Claude to himself. That was something at least.

They followed them back into the hotel and eventually to a meeting room, situated off the reception area.

The Sergeant plunged straight in.

'Brisbane Police have discovered an individual trying to make a concerted attempt to hire a contract killer.'

This was greeted by stunned silence.

'When? A year ago?' asked Claude, eventually.

'Nope, this week.'

'But . . . presumably not related to The Farm?' asked the manager, nervously.

'I'm afraid it is.'

More stunned expressions.

The Sergeant consulted his notebook. The man's name was Nathan Harvey, he said, and he'd apparently been asking every dubious character he could find in Brisbane whether twenty thousand dollars could buy a professional hit. But when he was arrested he immediately claimed he never had the money in the first place. He said he was only a middle man, acting for someone else.

'Acting for who?' asked Claude, struggling to believe the story. Had he seriously misjudged the situation?

'Wouldn't say,' the Sergeant went on. 'But the Brisbane police confiscated his phone and analysed his call logs. He'd been in regular contact with one phone, registered in England...'

He paused, presumably for dramatic effect.

'... belonging to a Mrs Marjorie Watson.'

Shocked, Claude and the manager swung round to Marjorie.

She shrugged, seemingly as unrepentant as ever.

'Well let's be honest, someone had to do something to move the peanut forward,' she said. She turned to Claude. 'You remember I talked about my nephew Nathan? He said he'd be delighted to help with the investigation. And now we presumably know whether or not there is such a thing as an Australian hit man. What's the answer Sergeant?'

Marjorie's response didn't quite seem to have the effect on Sergeant Mackenzie that she was hoping for. His mood seemed to deteriorate even further. This was, he pointed out, a very serious matter. He'd had to have lengthy conversations with senior police officers in both Brisbane and Darwin about how to proceed.

'Look, we've come to a decision,' he said, ominously. 'Given your extreme age, we're not intending to prosecute anyone. But I'm afraid you and Mr Simmons will have to leave.'

'Where? The hotel?' Marjorie asked.

'No, Australia.'

It was her turn to look stunned.

'What? You're deporting us?' she asked.

'No we're not but we could do. Look, we want you to leave under your own steam. Preferably tomorrow.'

While these bombshells were being dropped, nobody noticed that Ellie Hartmann had positioned herself outside of the meeting room's open door. She listened intently and scribbled furiously.

◆ ◆ ◆

Sergeant Deacon stood in front of Chief Constable Selby's desk, clutching his iPad. The Chief Constable signed the document he'd been studying and looked up.

'Yes, Sergeant,' he said.

'Umm, I just wanted to give you a heads up, sir,' said the Sergeant, nervously.

The Chief Constable winced. He hated the two words "heads up", not least because they almost always seemed to indicate that some sort of pain was heading in his general direction. On this occasion, it most definitely was.

'What is it?' he asked.

'Well, you might want to prepare yourself for a

phone call from the Commissioner of the Northern Territory Police.'

The Chief Constable looked back at the Sergeant in horror. Now he was able to attach the pain directly to two more words: "Claude" and "Marjorie".

The Sergeant handed him his iPad.

'Perhaps you'd better read this, sir.'

The Chief Constable looked at it. On the screen was the front page of The Alice Advertiser. It read, rather hysterically:

"Defective Detectives Ejected!"

Underneath was a picture which had been photoshopped to look as if Sergeant Mackenzie was showing Claude and Marjorie a red card.

The Chief Constable read the article with increasing alarm. Not surprisingly it seemed to be Marjorie Watson who was the villain of the piece.

'A professional hit man?' he spluttered. 'Twenty thousand dollars? Asked to leave the country?'

He looked at Sergeant Deacon.

'I need a full report on my desk as soon as possible,' he said, crossly. 'And I want to know the moment they arrive back at Heathrow.'

◆ ◆ ◆

Marjorie apologised to Claude for the third time.

They were sat at dinner, staring ruefully into their drinks. Things were so bad that they'd even lost the will to bicker with Scott. To his amazement, they'd both ordered the Chef's Special without even needing to hear the florid description he had carefully prepared for them. He wandered off shaking his head, hoping they were going to enjoy giant mud crab in mustard butter.

The truth was though that, despite her apologies, Marjorie wasn't really very sorry about what she'd done. She had realised early on in her relationship with Claude that she was never going to able to compete with his ability to analyse a crime scene, an autopsy report or a criminal's motives. So she had had to develop her own approach. Whenever a case hit a brick wall, her technique was simple. She would run straight at the brick wall. Chief Constable Selby had described it slightly differently in the Unsworth case. 'You need Marjorie Watson,' he had said to Lord Richard Unsworth, discussing the fact that the investigation was well and truly stuck. 'She'll barge over a few beehives for you.'

Usually, it worked out extremely well and a way forward almost always appeared from the rubble she created. What had let her down in this case, she believed, was not her technique but the fact that the Australian police simply didn't understand her. Or to put it another way, she was completely unable to manipulate them in the way she normally did with the police at home.

'Is this the end of the detective agency?' she asked Claude, dolefully.

He thought about this for a second. On the one hand, he knew it was entirely futile to write Marjorie off. She would doubtless make a dramatic comeback because she always did; as ever, it was just impossible to predict how or when. On the other hand, there was no doubt that their spectacular failure with the Kenny case was a major setback for them. He wasn't looking forward to the debrief with Helen Peterson. Or with Chief Constable Selby, for that matter.

'We'll have to see if we're offered any more cases, I suppose,' he said. 'It's possible the personal recommendations might dry up for a while.'

He was the master of understatement when he wanted to be.

Their discussion was abruptly ended by the arrival of the mud crab. It was not only enormous but, as it transpired, it was largely a DIY meal. There were crackers and picks for extracting the crabmeat from the shell and finger bowls and towels to help manage the mess. Most important of all, there was a bib for each of them. Scott helped tie the bibs in place and Claude and Marjorie sat looking at each other.

'To be honest, I was hoping not to be wearing a bib for another couple of years,' said Marjorie.

They both laughed.

◆ ◆ ◆

Claude arrived at reception just before midday the next day, suitcase in tow. He sat down to wait for Marjorie, contemplating the bleak journey that lay ahead. They faced almost thirty hours of travelling and, worse still, they were going to be flying in economy. Marjorie had booked the flights the previous day and, with her bravado still slightly dented, had announced they could no longer justify flying home in business class. Claude had been forced to agree.

A member of staff walked past. He was carrying a wooden easel under one arm and a large printed board under the other. Claude couldn't read all of the writing on the board but he spotted something about "Red" and "Mining". The member of staff disappeared off in the direction of the conference room, just around the corner from the meeting room where they'd been torn off a strip by Sergeant Mackenzie.

After a minute or so a second member of staff appeared. He was carrying a life-size cardboard cut-out of a man dressed in a smart suit. The cut-out was horizontal and tucked under his arm. Claude twisted his head sideways to try and get a proper view of it as it passed by. He frowned, extremely confused.

He eventually got up and followed the member of staff towards the conference room. As he rounded the corner, he saw that the cut-out man was now standing vertically in front of the conference room door, stabilised by a cardboard rudder at the rear. He looked as if he was greeting a crowd of people with a welcoming smile. Next to him was the easel, now holding the printed board. It read:

"Red Earth Mining Pty Ltd
Shareholder Conference
January 14, 2020
Welcome"

Claude walked up to the cardboard cut-out man and stood in front of him, eye-to-eye. He couldn't believe what he saw.

'Can I help you?' asked one of the staff members, spotting Claude's odd behaviour.

Claude was distracted. 'Perhaps in a second.'

He turned and walked briskly back to reception. He grabbed his suitcase and laid it flat on the floor. He unzipped it and rooted around until he found what he was looking for – a large photograph of Stephen

Kenny, given to him by Helen Peterson. He returned to the conference room and held the photograph up against the cardboard cut-out man's face.

They were identical.

'Good grief!' he said to himself, out loud. 'After all that, it's a case of mistaken identity!'

The member of staff looked at him, perplexed.

'Did they hold their shareholder conference here last year as well?' Claude asked him, pointing to the announcement board.

'Well they were supposed to,' he replied. 'But in the end it was cancelled. The, umm . . . the murder happened the day beforehand.'

Claude walked back to reception again, still carrying the photograph. He found that Marjorie had arrived with her suitcase. She was deep in conversation with the manager about the details of the bill.

'Both of you need to follow me,' he said, urgently.

Claude walked back to the conference room yet again, followed by Marjorie and the reluctant manager. He stood next to the cardboard cut-out man and gestured towards him with his hand.

'I'd like you to meet Stephen Kenny,' he said.

'No that's Greg Perry, the CEO of Red Earth Mining,' said the manager assertively, still thoroughly disgruntled with Claude and Marjorie and feeling he could do without this latest performance.

Claude held up the photograph of Stephen Kenny next to the cardboard cut-out.

'They appear to be one and the same person,' he said.

Marjorie and the manager moved in for a closer look. The likeness was uncanny.

'Very interesting Mr Simmons,' said the manager. 'But I'm afraid we must complete your check-out if you're going to make your flight in Alice Springs.'

Perhaps the shock of Claude's revelation had caught him unawares or he was simply anxious about Red Earth Mining's conference possibly being disrupted for the second year running. They were, after all, one of the few clients who'd stuck with The Farm. Either way the manager had entirely missed the point. Claude was forced to ramp things up.

'Mr Beckett, you don't seem to understand the significance of this,' he said, sternly. 'Your murder case is now solved.'

Mr Beckett blinked at him. Marjorie was agog. This seemed to be another one of those moments when Claude suddenly leapt four moves ahead of everyone else.

'But there is a much more pressing matter,' he went on. 'In my experience there is almost always a repetitive pattern to murder. Clearly someone tried to kill your Mr Perry at last year's conference and managed to kill Mr Kenny instead. There is a very good chance they will try and make a better job of it this year. Where is Mr Perry?'

Reality was dawning on the manager. He led them back to reception to consult with his computer. He scrolled through several pages and peered at the screen. He was due to arrive tomorrow, he said.

'And where is he now?'

This was something the manager knew the answer to. Mr Perry owned a retreat to the north east of The Farm, up beyond the MacDonnell mountains. He had arrived there sometime earlier to have a quiet period alone, perhaps to collect his thoughts before the shareholder presentation. The Farm had been liaising with Red Earth Mining's head office in Adelaide and had been sending some presentation materials to him at the retreat for his approval.

'We need to ring him right away,' said Claude, still in urgent mode.

'Ah, I'm afraid that won't be possible,' the manager replied. Apparently, the location of Mr Perry's retreat was extremely remote and there was no phone signal. He seemed to take his solitude extremely seriously and there was no internet connection either.

Claude fired off the next question immediately.

'How near is Sergeant Mackenzie's police station to the retreat?' he asked.

'Miles away I'm afraid. It's in more or less the opposite direction.'

Claude looked at Marjorie. He weighed things up. 'We're going to have to pay Mr Perry a visit ourselves,' he said.

◆ ◆ ◆

Cameron had been due to drive Claude and Marjorie back to the airport at Alice Springs. Now he found himself driving them to the MacDonnell mountain range. Oliver Beckett had been extremely reluctant to let them go. The idea of one of his staff driving two octogenarian guests towards a potential shooting was not particularly his idea of good hotel management. He had tried to ring Sergeant Mackenzie in the hope that he might intervene. The Sergeant was out and apparently uncontactable. The real problem for him was that Claude and Marjorie now had the bit between their teeth. They thrived on dangerous situations and there was really nothing he could do to stop them. He stood at the hotel's front door, wringing his hands as they drove away.

Claude and Marjorie had at least agreed to keep trying to call Sergeant Mackenzie to let him know the situation. Phone signal quickly petered out but the Land Cruiser was equipped with a satellite phone, as were all The Farm's vehicles. After half an hour, Claude asked Cameron to dial the Sergeant's number and put the phone on speaker. It rang several times and a grouchy voice answered. The Sergeant had returned.

'Sergeant, it's Claude Simmons,' Claude announced.

There was the usual pause.

'Shouldn't you be on an airplane?'

'Look, there's no real time to talk but basically the Stephen Kenny murder is now solved. It was a simple case of mistaken identity.'

'What?'

Claude pressed on, urgently.

'It means that Greg Perry, the CEO of Red Earth Mining, may be in danger.'

Another pause.

'What?'

'Phone the manager at The Farm, he'll give you the details. And he'll let you know the map reference for Greg Perry's property. You need to set off immediately.'

The Sergeant had more than had enough. Regrettably, he lapsed into the vernacular.

'Look, I don't take orders from you two old farts. Turn the bloody car round now.'

Marjorie leant forward to interject.

'There's really no need for bad language, Sergeant,' she said, righteously. 'Pull yourself together. And make sure you get your arse over to the Perry property.'

Sergeant Mackenzie erupted. He set off on a long tirade that involved considerably more swear words. And considerably more colourful ones at that. After ten seconds he realised he was ranting at the dialling tone. Marjorie had long since hung up.

Cameron drove on. They had left the metalled road behind some time ago and were negotiating dusty tracks that were rutted and potholed. It was a slow and difficult journey which you would have called round-the-houses, if there were actually any houses.

Marjorie sat forward. 'You seem to know where you're going,' she said to Cameron, with an element of hopefulness in her voice. 'How much longer?'

'Aw yeah, I was up here two days ago. Had to bring some presentation stuff for Mr Perry.' He looked at them both in his rear view mirror. 'I'm afraid we've got hours yet.'

Claude and Marjorie sat back and watched the red desert scrolling past. To all intents and purposes, they could have been staring at the surface of Mars. After a while the landscape began to change. The MacDonnell mountains were starting to hove into view.

They skirted Gosse's Bluff Crater and drove on beyond Tyler Pass, eventually meandering their way between spectacular canyons and gorges. It would have been a magnificent sightseeing day out, but for the fact that they were rushing to avert a possible murder.

Claude leant forward, wanting to know more about Greg Perry.

'You've met him Cameron, what's he like?'

Cameron thought about it for a moment. 'Bit of a loner, I suppose I'd say. I mean, I've only met him the once but there didn't seem to be anyone else around. Just him and about four thousand acres.'

'And Red Earth Mining?' asked Claude.

Cameron shrugged. He only knew what he read in the papers, he said. They apparently had mines all over the Red Centre – in South Australia as well as Northern Territories. They were a huge exporter of minerals and precious metals, particularly to China.

'They're not everybody's cup of tea, though,' he added.

'How so?'

'Well, there are a lot of disputes about some of the mines desecrating sacred Aboriginal land. Some

people get extremely upset about that sort of thing.'
　　Claude and Marjorie looked at each other.

CHAPTER SIX

They eventually arrived at the Perry property. The house was large and constructed almost entirely in wood and stone. It was set back about fifty or sixty yards from the road and was immediately surrounded by a wall which eventually gave way to a fence that disappeared off into the distance. There was a large pair of gates that housed an intercom.

Claude and Marjorie clambered out of the Land Cruiser and walked up to the gates. They pressed the intercom and waited. And waited. Claude peered over the wall. It was starting to get dark and there appeared to be a single light on in the house. He pressed the buzzer again, this time for longer. Eventually, there was the distinctive sound of an intercom phone being picked up.

'Yes?' said an impatient voice.

Claude faced a dilemma. There was a great deal to explain and an intercom was hardly the best place to do it.

'My name's Claude Simmons and I think your life might be in danger Mr Perry,' he said, trying to get straight to the point.

'What?'

'We have evidence that a man was killed exactly a year ago because he was mistaken for you.'

'What?'

Claude and Marjorie looked at each other. They were starting to struggle with what appeared to be the default Australian telephone manner.

'We can explain everything if you let us in please, Mr Perry,' Claude persisted.

Mr Perry's pauses were slightly shorter than Sergeant Mackenzie's.

'Go away.' He hung up.

Claude summoned Cameron from the Land Cruiser. He explained the situation to him and Cameron pressed the intercom buzzer again. Nothing happened. He pressed it another four times before there was an answer.

'I do have a gun,' said Mr Perry.

'Mr Perry, it's Cameron Cole from The Farm hotel, I was here two days ago,' he said, speaking very quickly to try and beat the phone being hung up again. 'What you've been told is true. Your life might be in danger.'

After what seemed an age there was a loud buzzing

noise and the gates began to swing open. Cameron, Claude and Marjorie clambered back into the Land Cruiser and drove in. They parked behind the house next to a solitary Land Rover and Marjorie retrieved the cardboard cut-out from the boot. She tucked it under her arm and they walked back to the front door. Mr Perry was waiting for them on the porch. He was tall and slim and suntanned. They climbed the porch steps and stood in front of him. If he was surprised to be confronted by two octogenarians, one carrying a cardboard image of him, then he didn't say so. He stood in silence, seemingly inviting the new arrivals to explain themselves.

Marjorie stood the cardboard cut-out up in front of him.

'This is you,' she said.

Perry looked at her, now wondering if he really should have let the three of them in.

However, Claude had brought the photograph of Stephen Kenny with him. He stepped forward and held it up next to the cardboard cut-out.

'And this is also you,' he said.

Greg Perry's eyes widened. He took the photo from Claude and stared at it in disbelief.

'Who is he?' he asked.

'His name is Stephen Kenny and he's the man who

was murdered at The Farm hotel the day before your shareholder conference last year.'

Long pause.

'And when was this photograph taken?'

Claude explained that the photo was apparently about two years old. This meant that it was not just a remarkable likeness but that Greg Perry and Stephen Perry were also of a very similar age.

Further pause.

'You'd better come inside.'

Perry held open the screen door and Claude, Marjorie and Cameron walked in. In some respects the house was similar to The Farm – floorboards, beams, stone. But it was spartan and functional by comparison, with none of The Farm's over-considered design flourishes. He led them through into a room at the back of the house which seemed to be his study. There was a sofa and several armchairs and they sat down. He switched the light on.

Claude thought it best to properly introduce himself and Marjorie. He explained his own police background and his detective partnership with Marjorie. He briefly outlined several of their cases. From Mr Perry's expression it wasn't obvious whether this brought clarity or confusion to the situation.

'I'm assuming you've never met Stephen Kenny?'

asked Claude, trying to move things forward.

Mr Perry shook his head. He was still holding the photograph.

'I most certainly haven't.'

'And do you know anyone who might have a motive to kill you?'

He thought about this. 'Before we go any further with your cross-examination Mr Simmons, where are the police in all of this?'

Claude was keen to avoid discussing his and Marjorie's various run-ins with Sergeant Mackenzie. Choosing his words carefully, he told him that the police investigating the Stephen Kenny murder had been informed of the situation. He also told him that they should be on their way to the Perry property now. With particular emphasis on the word "should".

'And in the meantime you really think I might be in danger?' Perry asked.

'I'm afraid I do.'

He got up and walked to a large wooden cabinet. He opened it and revealed that it housed, among other things, a safe. He stepped in front of it to hide the combination as he unlocked it. Marjorie had assumed he was bluffing when he had said earlier that he had a gun. Evidently he wasn't. He reached into the safe and produced a Glock pistol. She watched, fascinated, as he loaded it with a clip of bullets and double checked the safety mechanism. He returned to his chair and sat back down. He calmly laid the gun on the table next to him.

'So there have been threats to your life, then?' asked Claude, looking at the gun.

'Oh yes. When you're the CEO of a mining corporation with, how can I put it? . . . a large environmental footprint, then you're pretty much fair game for everyone.'

Back in Adelaide, he went on, he had a security detail that followed him around everywhere. He didn't like it but he had learned to live with it. Up here in this remote part of Northern Territories he had taken the decision that he would rather fend for himself.

Claude asked him if he and his security detail had been able to identify any specific threats.

Perry thought about this for a moment. 'The death threats are almost always anonymous,' he said. 'But there's one group that really has been disruptive in the last few years. They like to call themselves the RSA – the Real Soul Of Australia. We've got a more appropriate name for them but . . .' He looked at Marjorie, presumably thinking he should spare her any bad language.

He went on to explain that the RSA were responsible

for numerous acts of protest, vandalism and the frequent sabotage of mining equipment.

He was interrupted by Marjorie who burst out laughing.

'I've worked it out,' she said, triumphantly. 'The R Soul Of Australia.' She beamed at Perry.

Claude ignored her. He was keen to question Perry further. He remembered the comment that Cameron had made earlier in the car.

'But they presumably think you've been vandalising Aboriginal land, don't they?' he asked.

Greg Perry looked at him, slightly taken aback. He set off on a defensive justification of Red Earth Mining's actions. They were now one of Australia's largest corporations and its third largest exporter, he said. They went out of their way to avoid collateral damage to surrounding areas but some unintended consequences were inevitable.

Claude didn't believe a word of it. He pressed on nonetheless.

'So presumably the RSA is largely made up of . . . ?' He paused, not wanting to use the wrong phrase.

'Indigenous peoples?' said Cameron, helping out.

Claude nodded to him, gratefully.

'That's my point,' said Perry, fighting back. 'There's not a single indigenous person among them. They're nothing more than a white, middle class cult. They play at being hunters and gatherers with all sorts of self-righteous rules about minimum environmental impact. Then they drive to the nearest town in their 4x4 every Friday for a top-up shop.'

Claude looked at Perry, surprised at the level of his vitriol.

The intercom buzzer sounded.

It was very likely the police but Greg Perry picked up his gun nonetheless. He walked through to the lounge. It was now dark and he switched on the light. He peered out through the screen door as he picked up the intercom phone.

There was a sudden, loud crack of a rifle shot.

Greg Perry crashed to the floor. He moaned and writhed in pain. He clutched at his stomach with both hands. Blood seeped from the wound.

Marjorie was completely disorientated by the gunshot and Perry's collapse. She wasn't sure if events had rapidly speeded up or were now taking place in slow motion. She had a loud ringing in her ears.

Claude, by contrast, swung into action. He rushed into the front room and turned off the light, attempting to take away the shooter's advantage. He called for Cameron to help him. Together they dragged Perry back away from the door.

Marjorie followed them into the front room. In the darkness, she kicked something heavy on the floor. She bent down to investigate it. As she stood back up there was the distinctive sound of footsteps on the porch outside. She backed away blindly.

For just a moment, the world seemed to stop. Then the screen door was flung open. The light was switched back on. It revealed a man in his mid-twenties, focused and intense. He carried a rifle. He scanned the room and found two people standing next to Perry, one of them in his eighties. In the corner of the room was another eighty year old, standing with her hands behind her back. Confusion flickered across his face briefly. Perry remained on the floor, trying to support himself on one arm. He grimaced in pain. The gunman stepped forward and pointed the rifle at him, choosing to ignore the others. He had more bullets for them if necessary.

'You have violated the indigenous peoples of Australia and their sacred lands,' he said. It sounded awkward, as if it had been written by someone else and he'd had to learn it off by heart. 'For your own gain you have polluted the earth, the sky and the water. You have been judged and found guilty.'

Cult indeed, thought Claude.

The gunman took aim at Perry.

Marjorie produced the Glock pistol from behind her back. She had the strange sensation of being on autopilot even though she had never fired a gun before. She raised the pistol up and took aim at the gunman. Without hesitating, she fired.

The bullet struck the gunman in the upper arm, shattering the bone. He cried out in pain and dropped the rifle on the floor.

Claude stepped in immediately and picked up the rifle, a .308 Winchester. He turned to look at Marjorie. The report of the Glock had jolted her backwards and she had fallen onto a sofa. She lay there, the ringing in her ears now ten times as loud.

'Excellent shot, Marjorie,' he said, breaking the tension.

She hoisted herself up into a sitting position.

'Not really. I was aiming for his head.'

Claude immediately took charge. He prised the Glock from Marjorie and put it into his jacket pocket. Then he pointed the rifle squarely at the gunman while he sent Cameron off to find the property's first aid kit. Between them they managed to dress the wounds with lint and bandages. Greg Perry had been shot in the left side of his stomach and, while there was not inconsiderable blood loss, it looked as if the bullet had gone straight through and not struck any vital organs. The first aid kit also contained some codeine tablets and Claude offered them to Perry. He gratefully accepted.

Claude improvised a sling for the gunman. He asked him his name and got no response. He asked him if he was a member of the RSA. Nothing. He offered him the codeine tablets but he simply shook his head. Some strange sort of martyrdom, thought Claude.

Meantime, Marjorie was regaining her equilibrium. She was always quick to recover even, it appeared, after she had just shot someone. She moved straight on to practical concerns. They were stuck in the middle of nowhere with two people nursing gunshot wounds.

'What about the Flying Doctor?' she asked. She had been a big fan of the TV series. 'Is he still going?'

Cameron thought about it for a second. Yes, the Royal Flying Doctor Service was most certainly still going. But it was now pitch black outside and there was little prospect of landing a plane.

'Perhaps this is a test for the concierge at The Farm, then,' said Claude, joining in. 'I think we might be in need of one of those helicopters.'

Cameron went back to the Land Cruiser to find the satellite phone. He returned fifteen minutes later with the news that a large helicopter was on its way from

Alice Springs, complete with a medical team. It would take at least an hour and a half.

Everyone settled down to wait. There were still several ongoing problems that Claude was trying to wrestle with. First among them was the fact that the more time went on, the more the gunman became a flight risk. He had only been shot in the arm and could easily get up and walk off. Or, for that matter, run off. His car was parked somewhere near the front gate and he would almost certainly still have been able to drive. Of course, Claude had a rifle pointed at him, by way of dissuading him from any of those actions. But the question was, would he actually be prepared to use it? He briefly played out the brutality and likely illegality of that scenario in his head. Probably not, he concluded. Worse still, he knew the gunman would be in the process of coming to the same conclusion.

He had what he thought was a better idea. He reached into his pocket and found the Glock. He toyed with it briefly. Then he took it out of his pocket and gave it back to Marjorie.

'Right Marjorie, I want you to keep this trained on our friend here,' he said, pointing to the gunman. 'And if he tries to move, shoot him again.'

She took the gun and followed Claude's instructions, nonetheless astonished. This was entirely reckless and completely out of character for Claude.

The truth was, he had been forced make a cold-blooded calculation. The gunman had already been shot once by Marjorie and he had no reason to believe she wouldn't do it again. More to the point he knew she was a terrible shot and might actually hit him in the head this time, particularly if she was aiming for his leg. She was literally a loose cannon. He looked back at her, not daring to move a muscle.

Claude sat down next to Greg Perry. For some reason he was keen to know more about his background. The codeine tablets were starting to take effect and Perry seemed happy to try and chat for a while.

'Presumably you were born in Australia?' asked Claude.

'No, I was actually born in Stevenage in the UK. That's what my birth certificate says, anyway. My mother brought me here when I was three months old.'

Claude looked surprised. He asked about his father.

'How can I put it? He didn't make the journey with us.'

He went on to describe what had obviously been a difficult childhood. His mother had suffered from mental health issues and started to drink heavily. By the time he was six she was in and out of hospital and he had to be regularly taken into care. His mother eventually died when he was ten and his life became a succession of foster homes and orphanages.

'People accuse me of being a loner,' he said, candidly. 'The truth is, I just got rather good at looking out for myself.'

Suddenly, the helicopter could be heard approaching. It circled overhead for a while, using its powerful searchlights to find a flat piece of ground. In an enormous flurry of red dust, it landed. The medical team disembarked and hurried inside to tend to the injured.

Claude and Marjorie watched as they re-dressed the wounds, set up drips and administered more pain relief. Eventually, they stretchered Greg Perry out towards the helicopter. This presented Claude with a new concern. Actually, it was a variation of the old concern. Should he allow Greg Perry and his would-be-assassin on the same helicopter together, accompanied only by a medical team? Did this mean Claude would have to ride in the helicopter with them? Armed with a rifle he was reluctant to use?

Fortunately, the decision was taken out of his hands by the belated arrival of Sergeant Mackenzie. This could now be his responsibility, particularly as he had brought his Constable with him. They both got out of the police car and surveyed the scene.

'Good to see he's taking it seriously at last,' said Marjorie, bitingly. 'He's brought the whole police station with him.'

She was still smarting from her treatment by the Sergeant. She now had him very much in her gun sights, as it were. He walked up to them with a look of bewilderment on his face.

'What the hell's been going on here?' he asked, aggressively.

'Glad you could finally make it,' said Marjorie, wading straight in. 'Don't worry, while you were off rounding up a loose sheep, the old farts have cracked it for you.'

◆ ◆ ◆

Sergeant Deacon walked into the Chief Constable's office looking distinctly nervous. The Chief Constable glanced up from his desk. He was hoping that the Sergeant had some good news for him for a change.

'Have Claude and Marjorie landed?' he asked.

'Not as such,' said the Sergeant.

Now it was the Chief Constable's turn to be nervous. He demanded to know the reason for the change of plan.

Under the circumstances, the Sergeant thought it might be best to give him the answer in instalments.

'Actually, they haven't even boarded a plane yet, sir.'

'What? Why?'

'Umm, partly because Mrs Watson has been arrested.'

The Chief Constable had lurched from anxiety to shock.

'Arrested? For what?'

'Well, amongst other things, she seems to have shot someone.'

CHAPTER SEVEN

Events continued to move at a fast pace. Given the circumstances, Cameron organised a second helicopter for Claude and he eventually arrived back at The Farm, minus Marjorie.

He immediately picked up the phone and called Chief Constable Selby in the UK. He had to endure a considerable amount of shouting and a certain amount of swearing before he was able to get a word in edgeways. Eventually, the Chief Constable calmed down and Claude was able to brief him about what had really happened. He explained about their breakthrough in the Stephen Kenny case and their subsequent dash to Greg Perry's house. He told him about Marjorie's heroic act in saving Perry's life by wielding, of all things, a Glock pistol. He confessed to having fallen out very badly with Sergeant Mackenzie about her subsequent arrest.

'I think it's fair to say that relations between the Sergeant and I have now officially broken down,' said Claude, with considerable understatement. 'Which means there's some further information you might need to relay to the Northern Territory Police, please. Mackenzie almost certainly won't have done it yet, if he's going to do it at all.'

It was extremely late in Darwin, but the Chief Constable managed to eventually track down the Commissioner of the Northern Territory Police. He passed on to the startled Commissioner all of Claude's information about the murder of Stephen Kenny, the attempted murder of Greg Perry and, most importantly, the probable involvement of The Real Soul Of Australia. He added in Claude's speculation that ballistics would likely show the .308 Winchester rifle to be the weapon behind both shootings. He finished with a polite protest about Marjorie's arrest.

At eight o'clock the next morning, the Darwin police raided The Real Soul Of Australia's commune, north of the MacDonnell Mountains and west of Katherine. Despite loud and angry protests from the group's members, they began a room by room search and quickly discovered a number of illegal handguns and a considerable amount of explosives. The group seemed to share an old-fashioned computer and when the police eventually got it going it revealed a long list of planned attacks on other public figures. Finally, they found a passport in one of the rooms in the name of

Robert Heller. The photograph matched the mug shot of the gunman that had been taken the night before. All of this constituted a major coup for the police.

◆ ◆ ◆

Marjorie and Sergeant Mackenzie had spent most of the previous evening and some of the night bickering through the bars of Marjorie's cell. She'd been arrested, he told her, while certain charges were being investigated. Illegally discharging a firearm and malicious wounding, for example. Needless to say, Marjorie was outraged and vehemently protested her innocence. She flung a long list of charges back at the Sergeant. Malicious ignorance, for example.

She awoke in the morning after possibly the worst night's sleep she'd ever had. But despite that, her spirits were comparatively undimmed. The truth was, she wasn't remotely bothered about being arrested and was already intending to wear it as a badge of honour. Indeed, she was proud of the fact that she had been arrested once before back in the UK, for trespassing and attempted burglary in the Rosemary Fuller case. She sat on the bed, reminiscing. She idly speculated about which country she might like to be arrested in next.

For Sergeant Mackenzie's part, he was simply out of his depth. His authority had been called into question a number of times and he had allowed his disgruntlement about that to cloud his judgement. Had he stopped to think about it he would have realised he had made a series of poor decisions. But instead, he had promptly decided to compound the error by jailing Marjorie. Now he was well and truly dug in. And the only way forward was to keep digging.

Claude arrived at the police station at about eleven, having been driven by Cameron in the Land Cruiser. He had been instructed by Sergeant Mackenzie to bring Marjorie's passport with him but he had not done so. He had no intention of contributing to Marjorie staying in jail for a moment longer, he told the Sergeant. Needless to say, this didn't help the Sergeant's mood.

'I can easily ask Mrs Watson to budge up and make room in the cell for you as well,' he said, metaphorical shovel in hand.

The phone rang. The Sergeant picked it up.

'Yes?' he said, far too loudly and much too irritably.

Claude watched him. The Sergeant's mood changed rapidly as he listened to the caller's voice. His eyes began to widen. He suddenly stood to attention, clamping the phone to his ear.

'Yes, sir ... of course, sir,' he said, now sounding like reasonableness itself.

He listened intently to what was obviously a long and detailed lecture.

'I will indeed, sir,' he said, eventually. 'I'll tell her your exact words.'

He put the phone down. He was trying hard not to look shocked. He leant over the station's counter and took a set of keys hanging from a nail on the wall. He walked to the station's only cell and unlocked it. Marjorie had been sitting on the bed. She stood up.

'You're honoured,' he said. 'That was the Commissioner of the Northern Territory Police himself on the phone.' He paused, wrestling with the next part of the message. 'He's instructed me to release you. And he wants me to apologise on his behalf for the misunderstanding and any inconvenience you've been caused.'

Marjorie got up and walked to the cell door. She looked the Sergeant in the eye, not intending to let him off the hook.

'But what do you think, Sergeant? Are you apologising as well?' she asked.

He paused. He was now standing in a very deep hole. He looked at Claude and then back at Marjorie.

'I think you're bloody lucky to have friends in high places,' he said.

Marjorie gave up. Having now spent some hours with the Sergeant, she knew that this was the closest he was ever going to get to admitting he was in the wrong.

She and Claude walked out of the police station and into the rising heat. The town itself comprised one main road, surrounded by a sprawl of houses and bungalows, most of them with colourful, corrugated metal roofs. Apart from the police station, there was a petrol station, a hardware store, a supermarket which doubled as a post office and a hotel which doubled as a pub. Marjorie looked at the pub.

'Let's have a drink to celebrate,' she said. 'We might see a bit of authentic Australia for a change.'

They signalled to the waiting Cameron that they'd be ten minutes and crossed the road. The building appeared to be Victorian and was wrapped around by a wrought iron balcony, slightly in need of fresh paint. Inside, it was gloomy and smelt a little of yesterday's food. Three ceiling fans whirled manically, desperately trying to make up for the lack of air conditioning. A large flat screen TV on the wall was switched on and seemed to be showing nothing but horse racing. They looked around. There was only one other customer. He sat at the bar wearing shorts and a singlet, immobile behind a pint of lager. It wasn't entirely clear if he was an early starter that morning or a late finisher from the night before.

Claude and Marjorie perched themselves at the bar and the landlord appeared. He looked surprised to see two octogenarians sat in front of him.

'Good morning,' he said, putting on his politest voice for the newcomers. 'We don't often get tourists in here. What can I get you?'

Marjorie was feeling bullish after her recent exploits. 'We're not tourists,' she said. 'We're detectives and we're celebrating the fact that we've just solved a local murder.'

'Yeah, right!' said the landlord, laughing.

Marjorie and Claude stared back at him, stony faced. They were getting fed up with this default Australian reaction as well.

'Anyway, I'll have a gin and tonic, please,' she said, deciding to rise above it. 'And . . .' She turned to Claude who was surveying the beer pumps on the bar.

'And a Victoria Bitter, please,' he said.

The landlord watched Claude and Marjorie closely as he poured their drinks. He cast an anxious glance towards the door. Perhaps they'd given their carer the slip?

Marjorie sipped her drink.

'There's one thing I still don't understand, Claude,' she said. 'Why on earth did you give me back the gun at Perry's house and tell me to shoot the gunman if necessary? It's the most un-Claude-like thing you've ever done. I mean, I know your nickname in the Met was Psycho Simmons, but crikey . . .'

Claude put his hand in his jacket pocket and pulled out the Glock's clip of bullets. He put it on the bar.

'Thanks for reminding me,' he said, coolly. 'I must let Mr Perry have his bullets back.'

'What? . . . It was never even loaded?' said Marjorie, taken aback.

The landlord listened to the debate in disbelief. He briefly thought about calling Social Services.

When they eventually made it back to The Farm, they spent the remainder of the day enjoying something of a victory lap. To begin with, they were greeted enthusiastically on their return by the manager. This was a first. Clearly the events of the last twenty four hours had finally sunk in with him and, for once, he wore a smile. He led them through to the air conditioned comfort of the bar and ordered them afternoon tea, with the compliments of the hotel. They sat quietly, enjoying the improvement in their fortunes. Eventually, Marjorie turned on her phone and googled The Alice Advertiser for the latest splash. It read:

"Dead-Eyed Detective Shoots Assassin"

Underneath the racy headline was another photograph of Claude and Marjorie. She had been photoshopped to look as if she was carrying a machine gun and wearing a belt of bullets.

'My scrapbook's going to be full to bursting at the end of this,' she said, looking extremely pleased with the image.

After a well-earned afternoon nap they eventually regrouped for dinner at the restaurant. Even Scott was pleased to see them. The temperature had dropped to a pleasant twenty three degrees and he'd organised for their table to be set outside in the garden, next to a magnificent purple bougainvillea. Marjorie requested the wine list. She ordered the usual gin and tonic for herself and, after a brief deliberation, chose an extremely expensive bottle of Barossa Valley Shiraz for Claude. She was definitely back in her stride.

They sat chatting for a while before Marjorie eventually had a realisation. They hadn't had to suffer Scott's ritual reciting of the chef's special. Come to think of it, they hadn't even been offered menus.

Five minutes later, Scott reappeared, accompanied by a man who looked as if he could be the chef. They each carried a dish covered by a silver cloche. They placed one in front of Claude and one in front of Marjorie.

'Tonight, chef Andre has personally prepared two meals especially for you.' Scott announced, proudly.

The chef stepped forward and removed the two cloches with a deliberate flourish.

'Eh voila!' he said.

He revealed fish fingers, chips and peas for Marjorie and spaghetti Bolognese for Claude. Perfect.

◆ ◆ ◆

Claude felt strongly that he hadn't finished with the case yet. In any event, he and Marjorie had decided to stay another couple of days at The Farm before travelling home. This would hopefully give him time to investigate things a little further and offer them both the opportunity to explore the area a little more. It would also give Marjorie more time to decide on the question which was preoccupying her: since they were going to be arriving home in triumph, should they fly first class or business class?

They enjoyed a leisurely breakfast and then met up with their guide. He had already collected their hamper for them and together they set off for a day trip to Kings Canyon.

'I ordered a pork pie and some scotch eggs,' said Marjorie. 'That should have set the two star chef another little test.'

Kings Canyon was known as one of the most spectacular locations in Australia, and with good reason.

Like so many other geological features in the region it was formed of red sandstone, but this time in the shape of sheer cliffs, plunging down one hundred metres to a valley of palm trees, water holes and rich vegetation. The best way to view the Canyon was on foot, in a three or four hour trek. Given that the temperature was edging up towards thirty six and that Claude and Marjorie were each edging up towards eighty two, they were happy to enjoy the view from the air conditioned comfort of the 4x4, with occasional stops at strategic vantage points.

The guide found a suitable spot for lunch. He brought out folding chairs and a table and opened up a large sun umbrella. There was white wine for Claude and, in its own small Thermos flask, a pre-mixed gin and tonic for Marjorie. The food was worthy of a good picnic at Royal Ascot. The pork pie was traditional and hearty, as were the scotch eggs. There was cold roast chicken and, instead of prawns, the Australian speciality of Moreton Bay Bugs. There was a proper salad, not just of garden leaves but also of tomatoes, cucumber and radishes. Somehow they'd managed to find two punnets of fresh strawberries, accompanied by fresh double cream. Marjorie was delighted. She was convinced she was bending The Farm's kitchen to her will.

They drove back slowly, taking in as much as they could of the rest of Watarrka National Park. When they eventually returned to the hotel it was beginning to get dark. They pottered around for a while. Given the extent of the lunch they had enjoyed they were in no hurry to rush to dinner. They finally made their way to the restaurant at nine and each ordered just a starter.

Marjorie checked her phone. An email had arrived from Helen Peterson. It read:

"Dear Claude and Marjorie,

I have just heard the wonderful news from Sergeant Deacon that Stephen's murder has finally been solved. I wanted to email immediately to thank you and to congratulate you both.

As ever, I am waiting on the Australian police. When they finally acknowledge that I am no longer a suspect, I will immediately transfer your £10,000 reward to you. Please forward me your bank account details in anticipation.

Thank you again.

Helen Peterson"

'What a lovely email to receive,' Marjorie remarked. 'I always said I liked her.'

Their starters arrived and they prodded them around their plates for a while. Marjorie was daydreaming.

'What will you spend your share of the loot on?' she asked. 'I'm thinking about a diamond studded Zimmer frame.'

Claude smiled. He had not the first idea what he would do with the money and decided to sidestep the question.

'To be honest,' he said, 'I'm much more focused on our one dollar bet. When are you planning to pay up?'

'Me pay up?' she said, feigning outrage. 'I've been waiting for you to pay up.'

'Marjorie, the murder is no longer random. We now know it was a simple case of mistaken identity.'

'But mistaken identity is just another term for coincidence, isn't it? And what exactly is the difference between coincidence and random?'

Claude thought about this. It was a little late in the evening for existential debate.

'Perhaps some more evidence will come along shortly which will make things a bit clearer for you,' he said.

'What on earth does that mean?'

They eventually called it a night and returned to their cabins. Claude calculated that it was still mid-afternoon in the UK. He turned on his phone and rang Sergeant Deacon. The Sergeant had remained in contact with the Australian police and accordingly had several pieces of news about the case. Claude, in turn, had a number of things that he wanted to discuss with Sergeant Deacon. He settled back and they chatted for about twenty minutes.

In the morning, Claude and Marjorie had a late and leisurely breakfast of bacon, eggs and plum tomatoes. Afterwards, Marjorie went off with her book to sit by the pool. Claude returned briefly to his cabin. He rang the hotel's reception and they managed to put him through to Greg Perry in his private room at the hospital in Alice Springs. First of all, Perry confirmed that his surgery had gone well and that the prognosis was for a full recovery. Then Claude had a few questions to ask him. Given that he'd just had his life saved by Claude and Marjorie, Perry was happy to try and answer. Even though the questions seemed slightly odd. After he'd finished the call, Claude dialled Sergeant Deacon's number again. It was now the middle of the night in the UK. He left the Sergeant a detailed message.

He sat thinking things over for a while longer before picking up his Bradman biography and heading for the pool. He sat down on a lounger next to Marjorie, under a large sun umbrella. Marjorie was squinting at her iPad in the bright sunshine, trying to ascertain the availability of flights home.

'I have some news about the case,' he said. She put the iPad down. 'Ballistics have apparently proved that the same rifle was used to shoot both Stephen Kenny and Greg Perry. And our gunman has now confessed to everything. You're about to come into some money, Marjorie.'

Marjorie seemed pleased, although slightly confused as well.

'How did you find that out?' she asked.

'Oh you know, I was just tying up a few loose ends.'

She now looked distinctly suspicious.

'Tying them up with who?'

Claude was saved by the arrival of the manager. He was wearing his cotton suit and a very broad smile.

'May I interrupt?' he asked, rhetorically.

He sat down on the edge of a lounger and explained that he had just been speaking to the CEO of the Elysium Leisure Group, the company which owned The Farm. The company was delighted that the murder had been solved and that the hotel's name had effectively been cleared. They were now planning a complete re-launch of the hotel in September and were already working on an extensive marketing plan.

'In the meantime,' he went on, 'they would like to offer you an all-expenses paid stay at their premier resort, by way of a thank you.'

Claude and Marjorie were taken aback. They looked at each other.

'And where would that be?' asked Claude.

'It's Elysium's only six star resort,' he replied, slightly pretentiously. 'It's called The Island Hotel and it's on the Great Barrier Reef, in Far North Queensland.'

CHAPTER EIGHT

Claude and Marjorie sat down for their final dinner at The Farm before they headed off for the Great Barrier Reef. Scott showed them to their table and everyone seemed keen to part company on a good note. In the spirit of Anglo-Australian cooperation, Claude and Marjorie went as far as to order the chef's special dessert: a soufflé, with saffron honey and orange ice cream. It was absolutely delicious.

They had just retired with their drinks to the patio when Claude's phone buzzed. It was Sergeant Deacon, wondering whether they might both be available for a FaceTime. Marjorie went back to her cabin to retrieve her iPad. She returned feeling rather anxious, fearing a conspiracy by Claude to relieve her of her Australian dollar. Her anxiety was justified.

'Good afternoon!' said Sergeant Deacon, as his image appeared on the screen.

'Good evening!' chorused Claude and Marjorie.

They began the conversation with an exchange of

pleasantries, including the usual British discussion about the weather – it had been thirty seven degrees beside The Farm's pool that afternoon and it was currently minus one outside Sergeant Deacon's police station. Sergeant Deacon seemed envious.

'Anyway, what have you been able to discover?' asked Claude, keen to move things along.

'It was exactly as you suspected, Chief Superintendent,' the Sergeant replied. 'Stephen Kenny's mother gave birth in St Albans general hospital on the fourteenth of August, 1974. Not just to Stephen Kenny but to twins.'

Marjorie looked from the screen to Claude, astonished. Her brain was racing to catch up.

'What? What are you saying?' she asked, incredulously. 'That Kenny and Perry were actually brothers? ... And she gave Perry away?'

'That's more or less what I'm saying,' said the Sergeant. 'But she didn't give him away. He was stolen. One of the twins was snatched from the maternity ward the night they were born. He was never found. I've emailed you both a press cutting about it from the local newspaper at the time.'

Claude's hunch had broadly been proved right but he remained uncertain about most of the details. Stealing a baby was an extremely irrational act and certainly accorded with Perry's mother's mental health issues. But how on earth did she then manage to smuggle the stolen baby into Australia?

He had found out a number of things from his phone conversation with Greg Perry and had passed them on to Sergeant Deacon. Perry's birth certificate did indeed say that he was born in Stevenage. This was about fifteen miles from the hospital in St Albans. The date of his birth had been listed as the twenty first of August, one week after Stephen Kenny's, and his mother was named on his birth certificate as Florence Perry. All of that now seemed to be a matter of public record. But the question was, how on earth had she been able to organise it?

Fortunately, Sergeant Deacon had been able to discover at least part of the answer.

'I've been doing a bit of hunting around,' he said, 'and I'm glad to say that Stevenage town council keeps excellent records, all neatly microfiched. Apparently, there was a Florence Perry who worked at Stevenage Town Hall in 1974. In the wages department. So my basic assumption is that she managed to somehow acquire a blank birth certificate while she was there. I assume she filled it in and simply wrote down Greg's date of birth as a week later than Stephen Kenny's. To try and cover her tracks I imagine.'

Marjorie interrupted again. She had been forced to abandon her concerns about her bet with Claude while she tried to understand the whirlwind of information coming her way. The sum total of her knowledge of falsifying documents came from watching spy dramas on TV where every double agent always seemed to have at least five fake passports.

'And it's easy to just acquire a birth certificate, is it?' she asked.

Claude and Sergeant Deacon were being forced to speculate and neither could be one hundred per cent certain that this was what had actually happened. But they both thought it seemed likely. Claude explained that, since Florence Perry worked for the town council, she could have simply stolen a blank birth certificate from the Registry Office itself. Or more likely paid someone who worked in the Registry Office to steal it for her.

'I don't want to sound overly cynical,' he said. 'But in my experience, if you have the money then almost everything is for sale.'

These days, the theft of such a document would be much more difficult, he went on. But back in 1974 there were simply no digital records to cross check things against. If someone had also been able to make a corresponding entry to the birth certificate in the

Register Of Births itself then everything might well have appeared to tally.

'And once you have a birth certificate, you're well on your way to having a passport,' added the Sergeant, neatly rounding off the argument.

The three of them fell silent for a moment

'Did Stephen Kenny know he had a twin?' asked Marjorie, eventually. This was a good question.

Sergeant Deacon had been very thorough with his research but, again, it had been difficult to find a definitive answer. Both of Kenny's parents were now dead and there were no other siblings to ask. However, he had told Helen Peterson that Stephen very likely had a twin and she was completely shocked. In fifteen years she said he had never once mentioned anything like that. In her opinion, it was impossible to believe that he knew.

'His poor old mother,' said Claude, thinking out loud. 'She was probably unable to speak of the loss afterwards. I think we call that PTSD these days, don't we?'

The conversation drew to a close and Claude and Marjorie thanked Sergeant Deacon for all of his hard work. They signed off.

Marjorie looked at Claude. He seemed pleased.

'Nobody likes a clever clogs,' she said.

◆ ◆ ◆

They set off early on the long journey back to Alice Springs, driven by Cameron in the Land Cruiser. Marjorie gazed out of the window wistfully. She and Claude had had their ups and downs in the Northern Territories but she knew she would miss it, not least the hypnotic beauty of the red desert. Now they faced a six hour flight to Cairns and an overnight stay. This would be followed by a three hour boat journey to The Island Hotel the next day. Vast red desert was about to be replaced by vast blue ocean.

To while away the time, Marjorie had a brief go at resurrecting the debate about Australian straightforwardness. She pointed out that it now wasn't just The Farm being so named because it used to be a farm. It was also The Island Hotel being so named because it was a hotel on an island. She seemed to find this endlessly amusing. Claude pretended to be asleep.

After what seemed an age, they started to approach the outskirts of Alice Springs. Claude, now most definitely awake, looked across at Marjorie.

'Will you be changing some money at the airport?' he asked her, in a slightly satirical tone. 'You know, so you can pay me the Australian dollar you owe me?'

Marjorie had been expecting this.

'Absolutely not,' she said. 'Despite you and Sergeant Deacon working against me, the situation remains unchanged. The murder was still a coincidence. Stephen Kenny just happened to be in the wrong place at the wrong time. Randomly.'

'Come on Marjorie. The murder is now fully explained by the fact that they were twins. Pay up.'

Marjorie thought about this.

'We need to go to arbitration,' she said.

CHAPTER NINE

The next morning, they were picked up at eight o'clock from the hotel in Cairns by a stretch limousine. The car was ridiculously ostentatious, with the driver wearing a chauffeur's uniform, topped off with a peaked cap. Marjorie had never experienced anything quite like it before and didn't know whether to be excited or embarrassed. Claude eyed the car up and down. He was just plain embarrassed.

They clambered in and sat down. It was cavernous. Marjorie was as fascinated with the gadgets and the luxurious features as she had been with her flat bed on the Qantas flight. In front of them on a padded leather table sat an ice bucket with a bottle of champagne nestled inside. Behind it was a large television screen. To one side, there were several built-in cabinets, their doors constructed of burr walnut veneer. She opened the first door and it revealed a small fridge full of beers, mixers and water. She leant further forward and opened the second. Inside were three cut glass decanters, one filled with whisky, one with brandy and one with gin. She settled back in her seat.

'Actually, I could easily get used to this,' she said.

They gazed out of the window at Cairns passing by. It was different from the red desert in almost every way – busy, built-up and quite commercial in places. It was also dotted with palm trees and tropical greenery. Brightly coloured parakeets congregated in the trees.

Claude was deep in thought.

'Now I want you to take this the right way, Marjorie,' he said, eventually.

She looked across at him. She had studiously avoided the gin decanter and felt she had done nothing else to be upbraided for.

'I think I've had enough of murder for the moment,' he announced, unexpectedly. 'So if it's alright with you, I think we should downplay the detective bit from now on. Just enjoy our time on the island.'

Marjorie thought about this. She was nothing if not adaptable. In any event, she herself had had enough of the incredulous "Yeah, right!" reaction whenever she tried to explain their credentials, particularly to Australians.

'Fine by me. Who exactly are we then?'

Claude paused for a moment. 'Well, husband and wife I suppose, if that's okay. It's a chance for another bravura acting performance from you, Marjorie.'

She had played the part of an absent-minded, frail old lady in the Rosemary Fuller murder case, in order to help ensnare a criminal gang. Her performance had been absolutely brilliant, right up to the point where the gang had kidnapped her.

She gazed out of the window as the pier and the waiting boat swung into view.

'Mrs Marjorie Simmons, very pleased to meet you,' she said, limbering up.

It wasn't entirely clear whether the boat should best be described as a cabin cruiser or a yacht. In any event, it was about forty foot long and extremely well appointed. Claude and Marjorie climbed on board and took up residence in the cabin. They sat down on a large banquette, upholstered in bright blue and white striped cotton. Around them, everything was trimmed with beautiful teak and finished in gleaming yacht varnish.

'Again, I could get used to this,' said Marjorie.

The boat could easily have accommodated a dozen people but there were just three other passengers travelling to the hotel with Claude and Marjorie. First of all there was Ian and Dawn, a couple from Melbourne, probably in their mid-fifties. Dawn, it turned out, could talk for Australia. The boat had barely left the harbour before she had regaled everyone with most of the details of her life story: Ian was a dentist (own practice, successful); they had three children (two boys, one girl, also successful); she was hoping to have as many grandchildren as possible (as yet, unsuccessful).

'And now we're off to The Island Hotel for the trip of a lifetime,' she said, positively glowing with pride. 'It's our silver wedding anniversary.'

Marjorie was rather bored with Dawn's story and had been waiting for a gap in the monologue.

'How lovely,' she said, jumping in. 'Of course, Claude and I are celebrating sixty years together. It's our diamond wedding anniversary.' She patted Claude's arm affectionately. 'Doesn't seem a day too long.'

She beamed at Dawn and Ian. She was enjoying her new acting role and was already feeling quite competitive about her notional marriage to Claude.

The remaining passenger was a woman in her twenties. Marjorie turned on her next.

'And what about you dear? What's an attractive young girl like you doing travelling to a desert island all on her own?'

As ever, Marjorie was following political correctness at a leisurely pace. Claude thought the question entirely inappropriate but, fortunately, the woman seemed unconcerned.

She was tall, blond and, it quickly transpired, quite self-assured. Her name was Alyssa and she was, she said, a fashion model. She apparently had a photo shoot booked on a nearby island the following week, modelling a major new range of swimwear.

'So I thought, why not spend a few extra days at The Island Hotel? You know, work on my tan a bit.' She stretched luxuriantly as she spoke.

Marjorie looked her up and down, trying to work her out. She noticed that she was wearing an expensive looking engagement ring. Yet there was no mention of a husband or a partner.

Claude got up and walked to the back of the boat. Marjorie joined him. Cairns had long since disappeared from view and they were now navigating their way through the seemingly endless maze of coral. They lost themselves for some time in the ultramarine and the indigo and the turquoise of the ocean. Eventually, an island appeared on the horizon.

◆ ◆ ◆

The captain steered the boat very slowly towards the beach.

'The island's like a perfect circle and completely ringed with coral,' he called back over his shoulder from the cockpit, peering intently at the water. 'Sorry, it means there's just this one channel in and out.'

Marjorie looked out of the cabin window. 'What's the actual name of the island itself?' she called out, sensing a teaching moment.

The captain paused, as if being asked to state the blindingly obvious.

'Well funnily enough, Circular Island.'

Marjorie turned to Claude and grinned. Claude stared back.

'Shocking,' he said, flatly refusing to play the game any longer. 'I could have sworn he was going to say Triangular Island.'

A small army of staff was waiting on the beach to greet them, each sporting a smart pink polo shirt embroidered with The Island Hotel's logo – a perfect circle with one big palm tree sticking out of it. They quickly tied up the boat and helped the passengers down onto the white sand. Luggage was collected and the five new arrivals were ushered across the white sand and through the gently swaying palm trees to the hotel where a welcome cocktail and the ubiquitous refreshing hot towel awaited them.

Claude and Marjorie sat by the pool sipping their cocktails. Actually Claude sat sipping his. Marjorie, as usual, had requested a gin and tonic and a member of staff had returned with it immediately. Meanwhile, she sat staring at the poolside bar, fascinated by its design. Basically, it was double-sided and whilst you could perch on a bar stool on one side and enjoy a drink in the usual way, you could also perch on a bar stool in the pool itself and enjoy a drink in a rather more relaxed way.

Another member of staff arrived at their table, carrying their room keys. Accommodation at The Island Hotel was arranged in the form of huts, dotted amongst the palm trees and the tropical flowers. They were constructed from local hardwood and thatched with palm leaves for maximum back-to-nature authenticity but, rather like the cabins at The Farm, were ruthlessly air conditioned and crammed with every imaginable luxury. Like chocolate covered macadamia nuts, for example.

Claude looked at the keys and then at Marjorie.

'Ah. Almost immediately I see the flaw in my new plan. We're husband and wife and yet we're staying in separate huts.'

Marjorie weighed this up. She was enjoying the prospect of her new role far too much to give up now.

'I doubt anyone will even notice,' she said. 'But if they do we can just talk our way round it. You know, play the eccentric English card or something.'

The staff member guided them to their huts which were adjacent to each other. They were about to open their respective doors when Ian and Dawn came walking past, carrying their own room key. They stopped. Baffled, they looked first at Claude in his doorway and then at Marjorie in hers.

Marjorie looked back at them both.

'He snores terribly,' she said, smiling bravely. She opened the door and disappeared into her room.

That evening the weather was fine and everyone dined outside. The Island Hotel, although boasting one more star than The Farm, was considerably more relaxed and informal. Actually, the hotel had had a brave try at maintaining standards by announcing on their website that their dress code was "elegant resort wear". But that was about as convoluted as "are you comfortable with your wine levels?" and no-one seemed to be taking it seriously. A brief glance at the diners that evening showed a strong preference for shorts, flip flops and t-shirts.

In the same vein, Claude and Marjorie were pleased to find that Shane, their new waiter, was affable and chatty. He explained that the hotel had a top flight chef and an excellent a la carte menu. There was even a chef's special if they were interested.

'But,' he said, leaning in and lowering his voice

slightly, 'you'd be mad not to try the barbie.'

They happily took his advice and listened attentively to the impressive list of meats and seafood on offer.

'I'm going to have to reluctantly settle for the whole grilled lobster,' said Marjorie, smiling.

Claude reluctantly settled for the same and Shane disappeared off in the direction of the barbeque. Claude and Marjorie clinked their glasses together, not quite believing their good fortune.

Yet another member of staff arrived, although this time not dressed in pink polo shirt. He introduced himself as Michael Hayden, the manager of the hotel. He smiled broadly.

'Welcome. You must be our distinguished detectives.'

Marjorie looked at Claude. She leant forward towards the manager.

'Sshh! We're travelling incognito.'

'Sorry?' The manager looked slightly alarmed.

Claude intervened. He tried to explain that he and Marjorie were basically done with detective work for the time being and were just intending to relax and enjoy their time at The Island Hotel. To all intents and purposes, they were hoping to simply appear to be Mr and Mrs Simmons.

'Ah, fine by me,' said the manager, laughing nervously. 'After all I don't want to wish a murder on us.'

Shane arrived with the food.

'Bon apetit,' said the manager and set off in search of Ian and Dawn's table, to offer them their welcome chat.

Claude and Marjorie tucked into the lobster. It was superb, having been slavered in garlic and herb butter before being barbequed. Best of all it was accompanied by a big bowl of chips, thoughtfully provided by Shane.

They finished the evening with a walk to the beach. Away from the ambient light of the outdoor restaurant and the hotel buildings, the stars were astonishing. The Milky Way blazed from the inky black sky and they stared up at it, feeling slightly overpowered. Claude had developed an interest in astronomy years before, when he had been trying to help his son with his A-level physics. He tried to impart what little knowledge he could remember to Marjorie.

'The slightly comical thing is, constellations we're used to in England are literally upside down here. So if you can find Orion the Hunter, he'll be standing on his head.'

Marjorie was struggling to work out how that could be but Claude hadn't finished.

'But the best sighting is right there.' He pointed his walking stick skywards at a particular cluster of stars. 'That, I believe, is the Southern Cross, the most famous...'

He was interrupted by a woman's voice, quite loud.

'I most certainly will not!'

It was coming from down near the water's edge, further along the beach. Instinctively, Claude shepherded Marjorie towards a nearby palm tree. They peered out from behind it and were just about able to make out a man and a woman, silhouetted against the starlight reflected in the ocean.

'I'm not sure if either of us ever had 20/20 vision, Claude,' whispered Marjorie, squinting into the darkness. 'But I think I speak for both of us when I say it's definitely 80/80 now.'

Claude couldn't disagree. But the strange thing was that, while they were unable to see clearly who the couple were, the couple's body language was unmistakable. They watched as the man appeared to repeatedly try and grab the woman's arms while she, in turn, tried to back away. He hissed at her urgently and insistently. There was no doubt he was trying to calm her down. Or restrain her.

The woman was definitely not playing along. She shook off his attempts to grab her. She almost seemed to be raising her voice deliberately.

'Absolutely not! None of this is my fault!'

Claude and Marjorie continued to watch as the performance rose to a crescendo. The man could no longer keep his voice down.

'Damn you!'

The couple turned away from each other and walked off in opposite directions. The man headed back towards Claude and Marjorie and the main buildings. He hurried past their palm tree, clearly lost in thought and oblivious to their presence. He walked back into the light and they tried to ascertain what they could about his appearance – tall and well-built they thought. He strode purposefully on towards a hut, a little way along from Marjorie's. He opened the door and quickly went in.

◆ ◆ ◆

Marjorie was up early the next morning and set off on a brief meander around the resort. She made her way down towards the sea and wandered around for a while. She was thinking about the arguing couple from the night before and stood at the water's edge, the waves lapping gently over her bare feet. Suddenly, she smiled.

She headed back towards the hotel and stopped

briefly in front of the hut she'd seen the arguing man enter. She made a mental note of the number and then headed on to reception. She was greeted by a smiling young woman, dressed in the obligatory pink polo shirt.

'Good morning. How can I help?'

'Good morning,' said Marjorie, affecting a slight Dowager Duchess accent. 'I chatted briefly with one of your other guests at the pool yesterday and afterwards I realised he'd left his book behind.'

'Okay. Would you like me to give it back to him?'

'Oh no, I don't want to be a nuisance, I can do it. In any case, he and his wife are actually my next door neighbours, in hut number six I think. All I wanted to know was their name, please. I do think it's so important to be polite, don't you?'

This complete pack of lies seemed to have exactly the desired effect on the receptionist. Without a second thought, she tapped away on her computer and peered at the screen.

'Of course . . . here we are . . . hut number six . . .'

She grabbed a notepad and wrote the names down, reading from the screen. She tore off the page and handed it to Marjorie.

'Glad to be of assistance.'

Marjorie made her way to breakfast where she

found Claude waiting for her. She helped herself to a bowl of fresh tropical fruit and yoghurt and sat down. She looked extremely pleased with herself.

'I've been doing a bit of research,' she said.

Claude looked at her suspiciously, wondering where this was going. She continued on.

'The couple we saw arguing last night are from hut number six. And their names are...'

She unfolded the note the receptionist had given her.

'... Don and Lynne Anderson.'

'Very impressive,' said Claude. 'Not that we're doing any detective work at the moment.'

Inevitably though, Marjorie had started him thinking.

'In any event, why are you assuming they were a couple?'

'Well, I just thought it was standard husband and wife bickering, didn't you?'

'Probably. But why would they go outside for all the world to see and hear when they could have a perfectly good argument in the privacy of their own room?'

Marjorie pondered on this.

'Not that we're doing any detective work,' she said.

CHAPTER TEN

Claude and Marjorie followed Richie down the beach towards the sea. They passed a circle of bamboo canes, each stuck vertically in the sand and loosely tied together with a length of string. They effectively comprised a makeshift protective fence. On the string hung a handwritten sign which read:

"Shhh! Turtle eggs!"

'The whole island is basically a Marine National Park,' explained Richie. 'We're affiliated with the Marine Institute at Sydney University and we send them recordings and data about all sorts of stuff. Right now we're all waiting on the baby turtles.'

Marjorie was already feeling over-awed and they had barely started the day. They walked on and came to the glass bottom boat which had been hauled up half onto the beach. They clambered in and Richie pushed the boat back off the sand. He jumped in himself and started the motor. They slowly puttered off towards the coral.

Claude and Marjorie had paid a visit to Watersports after Michael Hayden, the manager, had sought them out again. He'd sat down at their breakfast table that morning and helpfully taken them through all of the hotel's numerous pursuits, beginning with fitness classes, walking tours and bird spotting.

'But all of our signature activities are down at Watersports,' he'd said. 'Wander down and make yourself known to Richie Gilmour. He'll sort you out.'

They finished their scrambled egg and bacon and did exactly that. They met Richie and he turned out to be just Marjorie's sort of Aussie - straightforward, approachable and altogether genuine. She and Claude fell in step with him immediately and he took them on a quick tour of all of the facilities on offer. There was a literal flotilla of craft to choose from, including dinghies and catamarans, kayaks and canoes and even speedboats and jetskis. Every imaginable aquatic sport seemed to be catered for. Marjorie surveyed the water front scene, overcome once more.

'It's all well and good Richie,' she said, 'but I've made a solemn promise to my care home that I won't water-ski or paraglide anymore. Sorry to let you down. Scuba diving is a definite no-no as well.'

Hence the glass bottom boat, the pragmatic option for octogenarians. Richie steered them out over the reef and almost immediately a large brain coral came into view through the glass. It was followed straight away by a beautiful Elkhorn coral. Shoals of fish began to appear, some bright yellow, some vivid blue and others electric purple. In no time at all the sea below them was a riot of outrageous colour.

Marjorie was now in danger of data overload. She was happy to admit that the closest she'd ever been to anything like this was sitting next to the tropical fish tank in the waiting room of her local dentist. Now she had a whole series of questions for Richie, as did Claude. Actually, they had pretty much the same question over and over again, accompanied by lots of pointing.

'What's that?'

'What's this?'

'What's his name?'

'What on earth are they?'

'Who's he?'

Richie was clearly used to such reactions. His ever-patient answers were:

'Parrotfish.'

'Fan coral.'

'Maori wrasse.'

'Giant blue lipped clams.'

'Butterfly fish.'

And so on and so on until they'd eventually exhausted the Q&A. Everyone sat quietly for a while, lost in their own observations. Suddenly a larger fish appeared. It swam alone and seemed to be surveying the other occupants of the reef as it snaked in and out of the coral. Given the beautiful fish they'd already seen, it looked rather menacing. Marjorie found herself pointing again.

'There, quick. What's that sharky-looking thing?'

Richie peered down through the glass.

'That sharky-looking thing is a shark. A white tipped reef shark to be precise.'

Claude and Marjorie looked at each other, surprised. They scanned the ocean around them and saw at least three other hotel guests snorkelling, apparently unconcerned. They turned back to Richie, questioningly.

'Don't worry, he'd be pretty harmless,' he went on, in that reassuringly matter-of-fact way that Australians have. 'Much more frightened of us than we are of him. Anyway, he's tiny.'

They all watched as the reef shark swam away. It didn't look that tiny to Marjorie and she wasn't entirely certain she was reassured. Richie tried again.

'Listen, the reef's pretty safe. I mean, you'll never get a big, aggressive shark – what I like to call a proper shark – swimming in this far. Far too shallow. No way they can navigate safely.'

He hadn't completely thought this through. It begged an obvious question and Claude was quick to ask it.

'And what about outside the reef?'

'Ah.'

This was clearly information the staff were not supposed to volunteer to the guests. Richie tried to cover his tracks by turning the discussion into a safety lecture.

'The water shelves deeply out beyond the reef. I definitely wouldn't recommend swimming there. Certainly not at night.'

Claude and Marjorie weren't letting it go.

'Why?' they both asked at the same time.

Richie paused. He had backed himself into a corner.

'Tiger sharks,' he said, flatly. 'Eating machines. And they feed at night. Trust me, you do not want to go anywhere near them.'

This produced a long pause.

'Well, I'm adding "midnight dips" to my list of prohibited watersport activities,' said Marjorie, eventually.

They motored back to Watersports and Claude and Marjorie walked slowly along the white sand to the main resort. They sat themselves down at the poolside bar. It was now a balmy thirty degrees and they were ready for a drink. However, the barman seemed preoccupied. He was deep in conversation with another guest at the other end of the bar. It was Alyssa, the young woman with whom they'd travelled from Cairns.

'Bloody hell, my tongue's nearly hanging out,' observed Marjorie, impatiently. 'Unfortunately, so is his.'

Claude leant forward and peered past Marjorie down the length of the bar. Alyssa had draped herself decorously across a bar stool. She was wearing a swimsuit which slightly defied description. Although "striking" and "small" would have been good attempts.

'Well, she is, umm . . .' Claude petered out, not sure about the best way for someone in his eighties to describe an attractive woman in her twenties. He needn't have worried. Marjorie had one of her favourite Aussie-isms primed and ready.

'You mean she could kick the arse off an emu?'

'Well I didn't think I meant that,' said Claude, slightly taken aback. 'But I suppose I could have done.'

They waited a little while longer for the barman to acknowledge their presence, but to no avail. Marjorie rapped her knuckles twice on the bar top.

'Shop!' she called out.

The barman sprung into action, realising his error. He came rushing up to Claude and Marjorie's end of the bar.

'I'm so sorry, I didn't see you both hiding there. Please, what can I get you?'

He was tall and tanned, with sun bleached hair. He tried to make good the situation with a broad smile.

Marjorie decided to give him the benefit of the doubt, even though she didn't feel she'd been hiding. She ordered her usual gin and tonic and Claude settled for a beer.

He started slicing lemons and theatrically bashing at a block of ice with a ridiculous looking chromium plated hammer. At the risk of pushing his luck, he made a brief sales pitch about the bar to Claude and Marjorie, listing the extensive number of cocktails on offer. He swept his arm across the array of spirits and liqueurs, tropical fruits and juicer machines on the bar behind him.

'And if none of the classics takes your fancy, I can help you design your very own cocktail. Name it after yourself if you'd like.'

He grinned at Marjorie, thinking she was probably the target audience for this offer. She stared back, keen not to give him any encouragement. However, he was sure he saw a brief flicker of interest in her expression.

They took their drinks and found two loungers by the pool. They settled down under a pair of voluminous, bright blue sun umbrellas. Claude was starting to relax, delighted not to be weighed down anymore with a murder to solve. But, in truth, he didn't find it entirely easy to switch off. Decades of service in the Metropolitan Police had meant he had acquired a persistent habit of people watching and he found himself idly scanning the pool area, taking in the activities and interactions of the other guests.

The pool was large and several people were swimming laps, powering along with an apparently effortless front crawl. A young couple, very possibly honeymooners, were splashing around in the shallow end. After a while, they each hoisted themselves onto an underwater bar stool. Claude watched as the barman prepared them both a cocktail, with ludicrous flamboyance.

However, the main source of activity in the pool area centred on somewhere else: Alyssa's lounger. She had evidently returned to her hut for a quick change and now modelled a bikini. Definitely striking. Definitely small. Now she reclined extravagantly on a bright pink towel, soaking up the afternoon sun. From Claude's vantage point he watched as successive middle-aged men found repeated excuses - yet another trip to the bar, an improbable need for a fresh towel - to pass by her lounger. Most simply walked on past, attempting to look as innocent as possible. Others tried, mostly unsuccessfully, to engage her in conversation. Around the pool various wives sat bolt upright, looking reprovingly over their sunglasses.

Claude glanced over at Marjorie to see if she was enjoying watching these rituals unfold. The barman had now arrived to stake his claim and was, rather inappropriately Claude thought, applying sun tan lotion to Alyssa's back. Marjorie had finished her gin and tonic and was snoring gently.

They arrived at dinner that night, ready for a barbeque. They took a moment to deliberate as Shane recited the long list of possibilities, now including several catch-of-the-day additions. Claude opted for the giant king prawns and Marjorie chose a thick-cut rump steak.

'On a scale from still twitching to fully cremated, how would you like it done?' asked Shane.

Again, this particular question almost certainly failed to follow staff/guest protocols at The Island Hotel, but Marjorie found it endearing nonetheless.

'Somewhere in the middle please,' she replied.

Shane turned to leave but Marjorie called him back. She leant forward towards him, keen not to be overheard. He leant in as well, understanding the signal. Marjorie pointed discretely in the direction of another couple three tables away who appeared to be having an intense discussion.

'What can you tell us about those two?' she asked. 'Is it the Andersons?'

Shane glanced at them quickly. 'It is. Don and Lynne. Regulars on the island.'

He went on to explain that Don's father owned a large boat building company in Brisbane. Don was the sales director. Evidently, the hotel owned several of their boats, including the forty footer that had transported Claude and Marjorie from Cairns.

'The company's called, umm, something blue. Indigo blue? Midnight blue? Nope, sorry. Can't remember.'

He wandered off to organise their food.

◆ ◆ ◆

Claude stared at the enamel logo fixed to the back of the hotel's game fishing boat. It read CobaltBlue. He climbed up the boat's ladder, with a little help from Richie, and clambered aboard. Richie had offered the possibility of a day's deep sea fishing when Claude and Marjorie had finished their glass bottom tour of the reef. Claude hadn't been entirely sure but in the end Marjorie had dared him into it, rather pointedly reminding him that this might be his last ever opportunity to catch a big game fish. She had then promptly backed out herself, claiming she needed to stay behind and research their flights home.

One more hotel guest arrived and climbed on board.

'Claude Simmons, meet Frank Gough,' said Richie. The two of them shook hands.

Richie left them to it and climbed up into the cockpit. As with all game fishing boats, this was situated above the cabin, almost giving it the look of a crow's nest. The general principle seemed to be that this offered the captain a commanding view of the ocean and the big fish.

Making up the party of four was Kath, the deckhand. She cast off and Richie steered the boat slowly out through the narrow channel towards the deeper water.

The boat sped up as it reached the bigger swell and the two guests went to sit down in the cabin. Unfortunately, it soon transpired that Frank could boast for Australia. He told Claude, without needing to be asked, that he was a currency trader. He described in detail his luxury apartment in Brisbane and then moved on to his second property, on the waterfront in Surfer's Paradise. He barely drew breath in reciting his list of accomplishments, most of them financial. He was a bit like Helen Peterson, thought Claude. But without the charm.

Claude switched off. In his head he had already found the words "brash" and "brazen" to describe Frank. He was now idly looking for another to make up an alliterative set of three and was wondering if "braggartly" would be acceptable.

The boat's engines slowed down. Kath had been setting up the fishing rods and baiting the lines with multi-coloured lures. She now began to cast them out, starting with two rods at the back of the boat and then with one on each side. They formed a neat semi-circle around the fighting chair which sat ominously facing the stern.

'And now we wait!' shouted Richie from the cockpit.

Wait they did. This was clearly a stretch of water that Richie regularly fished and he slowly motored round and round. But after nearly two hours there were still no bites. Even with an ocean apparently teeming with fish and a well equipped boat, fishing required a great deal of patience. Not that anyone seemed to have told Frank. He had expectantly sat himself in the fighting chair an hour earlier. He was starting to get grumpy.

Three seabirds flew past and Richie looked up at

them. He steered the boat round to follow them and slightly increased the speed of the engines. Claude thought this a rather hopeful strategy but soon they could see more seabirds congregating up ahead. Five minutes later they arrived at what can only be described as a furore. The seabirds wheeled around raucously, queuing up to dive vertically into the water. The water itself seemed to be boiling with fish.

'Tuna!' announced Kath, leaning over the side. 'Feeding frenzy!'

Richie had slowed down the boat again and cruised straight past the seething mass, dragging the fishing lines behind him. Almost immediately, one of the rods twitched and then arced towards the water. Line began to spool off rapidly from the reel. Kath snatched the rod from its mooring and handed it to Frank who was still sitting, somewhat regally, in the fighting chair. Between them they anchored the butt of the rod in the swivelling metal cup attached to the front of the seat and the fight began. For some time the fish battled bravely, taking more and more line from the reel. Until this stopped, there wasn't much Frank could do. Well, apart from boast.

'It's big!' he shouted.

Eventually he was able to start reeling the line back in although not without a lot of theatrical exertion.

He huffed and puffed and struggled and strained.

'Might not be a tuna! Feels more like a shark!'

Richie, with his commanding view of the battle, shook his head. Frank eventually brought the fish to the side of the boat and Kath helped him land it. It was a yellowfin tuna and weighed in at a healthy but not huge forty two kilos. Frank had his photo taken with the fish and then grabbed a beer from the cool box, as a reward for what he felt was his considerable achievement.

Richie motored towards a nearby reef and they anchored in the shallow water. He clambered down from the cockpit.

'Lunch,' he said.

Everyone sat down in the cabin and Kath opened the two large cool boxes. One contained drinks and the other contained food. They chatted over the chicken and prawns, mostly about Frank's cars and motorbikes. Eventually, Claude had a question to ask.

'What about this Don Anderson chap then Richie? He seems to have sold you a very nice boat.'

Richie was surprised at Claude's inside knowledge but pleased that he was being given the green light to gossip a little about the guests.

'Ah, both the boats are great. CobaltBlue is a fantastic make,' he said. 'I don't know Mr Anderson really but everyone says he's a smart businessman. Smart enough to have negotiated a free holiday for himself and his wife off the back of the sale, anyway.' He grinned.

'He's an arse,' said Frank, interrupting. 'I tried to buy a speedboat from him back in Brisbane but he wasn't having any of it. Made him a bloody good offer too. He's full of you-know-what.'

A bit rich coming from Frank, Claude thought.

They finished lunch and pulled the anchor in. Richie clambered back into the cockpit and started the engines. Kath put out the rods and they began fishing again. It was now the hottest part of the day and Claude and Frank stayed put inside the cabin. In any event, the heat seemed to have caused the fish to completely lose interest. Kath re-baited the lines several times and Richie tried successive fishing grounds but all to no avail. In the wake of considerable moaning from Frank they turned for home and began to fish their way slowly back towards the island.

Suddenly, the rod on the port side of the boat bent almost double. Line screamed off the reel.

'Whoa!' shouted Richie from the cockpit.

Claude scrambled his way towards the fighting chair and managed to sit himself down. Kath grabbed the rod and wrestled it over to him, managing to anchor it in the metal cup. There was nothing Claude could do but sit tight and try to hold the rod vertical. The fish continued to run.

Eventually, it seemed to relent, or at least pause for breath. Claude was about to start trying to reel it in when the fish suddenly leapt out of the water. It was a beautiful blue with a large bill and an enormous, fanned dorsal fin. For a moment it appeared to dance on the surface of the water with its tail.

'Sailfish!' shouted Richie.

Claude set about the fight. He had always kept himself in good shape and still exercised every day. But the reality was that he was now in his eighties. This was going to be a struggle. He planted both feet on the footboard and tried to find a rhythm, lowering the rod tip to reel in and then heaving it back to vertical again. He managed to keep going for five minutes. He had definitely made some progress but had to stop for breath. Kath administered some water.

He battled on again with the relentless task, feeling as if he was trying to reel in a ten ton weight. After a few more pauses for breath the sailfish leapt from the water again. At least it looked to be nearer the boat.

Frank was feeling distinctly left out.

'Listen Clive,' he said, 'if you need me to step in just let me know. Not sure this is a good idea for ninety year olds.'

Claude started to think about alliteration again. He thought of two words that went perfectly with "Frank", one of which was "off", and wondered whether or not to deploy them.

Fortunately, he was distracted by some encouragement from the cockpit.

'Come on! Nearly there!'

After struggling for another fifteen minutes Claude was completely done in but Kath had the fish by the side of the boat. Richie stopped the engines and came flying down the ladder. He looked over the side.

'Beauty! About fifty five kilos I'd say.'

After such a monumental battle, Claude was very reluctant to have the fish killed. They decided on Tag and Release instead and Claude watched as they tried to restrain it. It writhed and squirmed and thrashed around, flashing different colours of blue. It was quite the angriest thing he'd ever seen. Eventually they managed to insert the tag and the sailfish swam off, disappearing instantly into the depths. After several seconds it leapt out of the water one final time. It stuck its bill in the air, as if giving them the finger.

Richie revved up the engines and they set off for home. When they were about two miles from the resort they came to another, smaller island. It was basically just an outcrop of oblong rock jutting out of the sea. It looked inhospitable and uninhabited.

Claude was watching from the cabin. He looked at Kath. 'Let me guess, it's called Oblong Island.'

She looked surprised. 'How did you know that?'

As they approached the windward side of the island, they saw that the oblong rock gave way to a small strip of sand. On it was beached a bright yellow kayak.

'One of ours,' shouted Richie from the cockpit.

He circled the boat around the island quickly to check that there wasn't a stranded kayaker somewhere. There wasn't. Then he slowly motored in as close to the beach as he could and Kath dropped anchor. He climbed down from the cockpit and hunted out a length of rope from one of the boat's lockers. Kath took one end and jumped into the water. It was waist deep and she waded towards the kayak. She tied one end of the rope to its prow and Richie tied the other to the stern of the CobaltBlue.

'It's a fairly normal occurrence,' he said. 'There's quite a big current that runs from Circular Island to Oblong Island. So when a guest capsizes in a kayak the boat usually ends up down here.'

'And the guest?' asked Claude, a little concerned.

'Oh, they're fine,' he said in his matter-of-fact Aussie way. 'Everybody has to wear a life vest so they just swim back to the beach.'

They finished the journey slowly, towing the kayak behind them. Arlene, Frank's wife, was waiting for them on the beach when they arrived. Frank held up his tuna triumphantly.

'At least someone's managed to catch dinner,' he said.

Claude set off to find Marjorie. He arrived at the pool bar and quickly realised that, while he couldn't see her, he could most definitely hear her. He walked round to the other side of the bar and found her seated on a stool in the water.

'Claude! Come and join us!'

She was almost certainly tipsy. In addition to that, she was wearing a swimsuit that appeared to be from the nineteen fifties. It seemed to be made from an extremely generous amount of material, some of which was heavily underwired. It looked as if it probably contained a corset bone or two. It was topped off with a bright yellow bathing cap, adorned with assorted rubber flowers in various gaudy colours.

'Barry the barman has been helping me invent a cocktail, haven't you Barry?'

Barry stood behind the bar, looking very pleased with himself.

'You'll never guess what it's called.'
'Go on,' said Claude, fearing the worst.
She paused for dramatic effect.
'A Marjorita!'

CHAPTER ELEVEN

Breakfast was always served indoors at The Island Hotel. Marjorie arrived wearing sunglasses nonetheless. She moved her chair as far away from Claude's fried egg and bacon as she could and sat down.

'Sorry Claude. Bit too much sun yesterday.'

Claude looked up from his meal and smiled. It wasn't entirely clear if he was pleased to see her or simply amused at her plight.

Shane didn't help matters by bounding up to the table.

'G'day!' he said loudly. 'And what can I get you on this beautiful morning?'

Marjorie winced.

'Two paracetamol please. Perhaps some white toast. Under the circumstances, I might have to finally give in and order some Vegemite.'

She poured herself a cup of black coffee and cradled it in front of her. She was slowly starting to feel better. The toast and Vegemite ultimately saved the day.

Eventually they finished breakfast and set off to return to their huts. However, they quickly stumbled across what could best be described as an incident, taking place beside the pool. A group of people were gathered around a table, most of them staff. Michael Hayden, the manager, was bending down to talk to a woman who was seated at the table. Claude and Marjorie recognised her as Lynne Anderson. She was wearing one of the hotel's bath robes and looked confused and dishevelled. Eventually, Mr Hayden stood up and headed back to the main building, passing Claude and Marjorie as he did so.

'What's happened?' asked Claude.

'Oh, she seems to have misplaced her husband. Apparently has no idea where he's gone.' The manager wore a knowing smile. He was clearly trying to give off an air of "nothing to see here". He lowered his voice slightly. 'Bit too much to drink last night, I think.'

Marjorie was slightly offended on Mrs Anderson's behalf. 'And what are you doing about it?'

'There's nothing to do. Perhaps they've had a tiff and he's gone for a swim to cool off. Who knows? I'm sure he'll turn up when he's good and ready. Anyway, I think Mrs Anderson's due a visit from the hotel's nurse.' He shrugged his shoulders and set off for his office.

Claude and Marjorie completed the journey back to their huts. They checked their phones, collected their books and headed for the beach. They procured two loungers under a large palm tree and settled down to read. Claude had now got as far as Don Bradman's farewell tour of England in 1948 and was enjoying every word of it. Marjorie was riveted to a cosy murder mystery set in a remote Country House, with each of the weekend guests being a possible suspect.

After an hour or more a member of staff appeared. He offered a plate of refreshing pineapple slices, with cocktail sticks for spearing purposes.

'Ah, the courtesy pineapple,' said Marjorie. 'Perfect.'

They tucked in.

'What's the situation with Mr Anderson?' Claude asked. 'Has he reappeared yet?'

The member of staff looked nervous. 'Umm, I don't think so.'

Claude and Marjorie looked at each other. They really had been trying hard to leave detective work behind.

Claude got up. 'Come on. Duty calls.'

Marjorie followed him back up the beach towards the hotel. They headed for the manager's office and passed their own huts along the way. Claude noticed that two cleaners were leaving his hut and were just about to enter Marjorie's.

They actually found the manager in reception, pacing backwards and forwards. He looked at them, his nervousness immediately increasing.

'I suppose you're going to tell me I have to do something?'

'I'm afraid I'm going to tell you that you have to do quite a lot of things,' Claude replied, 'beginning with an immediate search of the island. Mr Anderson may be laying injured somewhere.'

The manager shrugged in grudging agreement. He had been worried about alarming the guests but, given that most of them had seen Mrs Anderson's bizarre performance at the pool anyway, he had to concede this might now be the least of his concerns.

'By the way, where is Mrs Anderson?' asked Claude.

'Sleeping it off in the medical room I believe.'

Claude weighed this up. 'Good, let's keep it that way. And you need to stop the cleaners who are about to enter her hut. Lock the door and keep it locked, please.'

This was suddenly very dramatic and Marjorie looked at Claude in admiration. However, he hadn't finished.

'I presume you've got someone checking CCTV footage?'

Mr Hayden seemed put out.

'There isn't any CCTV. Our guests come here to relax and escape from everyone's gaze. Why on earth would we then spy on them? The policy is clearly stated on our website.'

'Is it indeed?' said Claude wearily.

They turned to go but Claude thought of one last thing.

'By the way, I think you should notify the Cairns police. They might not come out yet but I think you have to let them know the score.'

They returned to their loungers on the beach. Given the circumstances they found it almost impossible to relax. Marjorie was musing on the coincidence of she and Claude arriving at the Island Hotel and then possibly having a dead body discovered. She was convinced that Michael Hayden was only just stopping short of accusing them of causing the whole thing.

'Perhaps we're becoming like those detectives on the telly,' she said. 'The ones who seem to be followed around by murders wherever they go.'

Claude looked at her, confused.

'You know, there's that chap with the waxy moustache. Or the old spinster lady. They're always off to stay at a posh house somewhere, only to trip over a corpse the very next day.' She was warming to her theme. 'Or there's that policeman in the tiny village in the countryside. Midwinter or something. There's only about fifty people living there but they manage to have a murder every week.'

◆ ◆ ◆

Barry from the poolside bar was conscripted to lead a small search party across the island's interior. His team fanned out and worked their way through the undergrowth, calling out Don Anderson's name repeatedly. The island wasn't huge and after an hour they'd reached the other side. Nothing.

Richie and Kath took the speedboat and circumnavigated the island. There were a number of sandy coves and various guests had grabbed themselves a private beach on a first-come-first-served basis. Some sunbathed. Some snorkelled. But there was no sign of Don Anderson.

One by one the members of the search team returned to the hotel, each reporting in with a shake of the head. Eventually, Michael Hayden made his way to the beach and found Claude and Marjorie, still waiting patiently on their loungers. He had an update. A terse update.

'No trace of him. The Cairns police are about to set off. I'm afraid they'll be at least a couple of hours.'

Claude eventually got up from the lounger and

headed off for a walk on his own. He reached the waterline and paddled along, in and out of the gentle waves. A memory from his childhood had suddenly come back to him and he was turning it over in his mind.

The memory concerned a holiday he had had with his mother and father and his elder brother when he was about twelve. They had gone to North Cornwall and had, for once, been blessed with glorious weather. Claude had spent the first two days in the sea, trying his level best to learn how to body surf. But on the third day a small crowd had gathered at the water's edge. It seemed that a boy, apparently the same age as Claude, had been swept out to sea. This was in the early nineteen fifties, before the advent of life guards and no-one seemed to know what to do. Eventually, someone ran off to try and alert the local lifeboat crew. The whole scene had filled Claude with a cold dread.

This hadn't been helped by his father. Percy Simmons had himself been a policeman – actually a Chief Inspector in the East Sussex force. Unfortunately, his twenty five years in uniform had left him with a philosophical outlook that was far too world weary. But, in his defence, he had seen this kind of incident play out on the Cornish beaches a number of times before.

'I'm afraid he's a gonner,' he had said as they had

walked back up from the beach to the hotel. 'On his way to Bedruthan Steps by now if I'm any judge.'

'Percy, please,' Claude's mother had said. She had put her arm around Claude and tried to give him a reassuring hug. He had no idea what or where Bedruthan Steps was but his imagination was now working overtime.

Two days later, his father was reading the local newspaper at breakfast in the hotel. The main headline read:

"Missing Boy's Body Found At Bedruthan Steps"

'See, same every year,' his father had said, phlegmatically. 'Prevailing currents.'

Claude stopped. He looked out at the open ocean beyond the reef. He turned and walked back as quickly as he could towards Marjorie.

'Come on. We've got work to do. And we're going to have to start by telling the truth.'

He set off at pace again, this time towards Watersports. Marjorie tried to catch up, struggling in the soft sand.

'Sorry? What?'

Claude was searching for Richie and found him in his wooden office, seated behind a computer console. He looked up briefly as Claude and Marjorie entered.

'Sorry, I'm just cancelling all the bookings for the

day, given the circumstances.'

He tapped away on the computer for a while longer and then appeared to press one final key.

'There,' he said, getting up from the desk. 'How can I help?'

Claude paused for a moment, frowning. 'We've got a confession to make, Richie. Marjorie and I aren't actually husband and wife.'

Richie looked taken aback. As conversation starters go, this wasn't what he was expecting. Claude pressed on regardless.

'Can I ask, did you happen to hear about the murder and the subsequent shooting in the Northern Territories recently, out past Alice Springs?'

'Umm. . . oh yeah, the one that was in the papers? Solved by the two old fogeys?'

Richie looked at Claude and Marjorie. They both looked back at him.

'Wait . . .' Realisation dawned. 'No!'

Claude shrugged. Richie stared at him, disbelievingly.

'So you're telling me you're the one that actually shot the murderer?'

Marjorie took a step forward. 'No, that was this old fogey.'

This conversation could clearly have gone on all day

but Claude was impatient.

'Anyway, more of that later but right now we have to find Don Anderson. There's one place left we need to search.'

'Where?' asked Richie.

'Oblong Island.'

The three of them set off towards the speedboat. It was moored to a buoy some way off from the beach and Richie waded out to it.

This was the first Marjorie had heard of Oblong Island and she was captivated by the name. While they waited, she took the opportunity to lecture Claude yet again about the joys of Australian bluntness. He ignored her.

Fortunately, Richie quickly arrived with the boat and helped them clamber aboard. He set off for the island at a moderate speed, given the octogenarian passengers.

'What's your thinking then?' Richie asked Claude.

'Oh, I don't know there's much thinking involved.' As ever, Claude was being modest. But he was also wary of getting everyone's hopes up. This endeavour was probably a long shot.

'It's just that Don Anderson isn't anywhere on Circular island. Therefore he must be somewhere off Circular Island.'

'Go on.'

Claude looked at Richie. 'I'm assuming all your boats and boards and windsurfers are accounted for?'

'They absolutely are.'

'So in the absence of any other ways of leaving the island, that leaves us with a simple working hypothesis. Mr Anderson has done a very silly thing and gone for a late night swim. If he's then got into difficulties, for whatever reason, the current will have taken him down to Oblong Island.'

Richie couldn't disagree with Claude's logic. Marjorie was still trying to process it all, particularly the bit about currents.

'So . . . you think there's a chance he's still alive?' she asked.

Claude paused. 'There's a chance, yes. Theoretically, he could be sitting on the beach waiting for someone to come and pick him up.'

Actually, he didn't really think there was much chance of this at all. But he was keen to avoid sounding like his father.

They motored on for a while and Oblong Island came into view. Richie stood up and peered ahead.

'Lot of activity on the beach,' he said.

Claude and Marjorie strained their eyes to see. There seemed to be a profusion of gulls. Some wheeled around noisily in the air. As they drew closer they could see there were even more of them on the beach, jostling and barging into each other. The focus of their attention seemed to be some sort of round object on the sand. It rolled backwards and forwards with the waves and the gulls hopped and scurried after it.

Richie drove the boat right up to the beach, about ten yards away from the melee. This succeeded in scattering the gulls, leaving behind the object of their attention. Everyone clambered out of the boat and walked forwards to get a better look.

It was a human head.

Claude and Richie bent down for a closer examination. For some reason, Marjorie continued walking and made her way further up the beach.

Claude was keen not to touch the head for the moment so they were forced to try and examine it as it rolled around in the waves. Even so it was quickly obvious how badly damaged it was. To begin with, both eyeballs were missing. There were numerous lesions to the face and scalp and the flesh around what remained of the neck was torn and jagged. It looked pale and bloodless.

Claude had seen a number of dead bodies in his time but nothing quite like this. He looked at Richie.

'Tiger shark?'

Richie shrugged. He'd never seen anything like it either.

They were interrupted by a loud noise from behind them. They turned around to see Marjorie standing behind a rock some way off, almost bent double. She was, to use the blunt Australian word, chundering.

After a moment she stood up straight again, wiping her mouth with a tissue. 'Sorry Claude,' she called out. 'Bit of sea sickness.'

Claude turned back to the severed head. He knew there were some decisions he was going to have to make immediately. To begin with, there was the possibility that this was now a murder inquiry and they had to try and avoid compromising the evidence if they could. But was that actually going to be possible? Richie's speedboat had no VHF radio and, stupidly, they hadn't told anyone where they were going. It meant they could be hours and hours in the hot tropical sun before the police actually found them. Claude upbraided himself for forgetting so much of the basics.

All the while the severed head itself was being progressively compromised anyway, rolling around in the salt water and grinding into the sand. As if to accentuate the point, a large dollop of bird poo landed right next to it on the sand, delivered by one of the cawing and screeching gulls that continued to circle overhead.

'Damn!' said Claude, standing up. They were completely ill-equipped for the task in hand.

'We're going to have take this with us,' he said to Richie, pointing at the head. 'Anything on the boat we could use?'

Richie racked his brains. There were snorkels, masks and flippers. Some water skiing equipment. And, in a bleak irony, there was a first aid kit. But nothing for transporting severed heads.

'Ah,' he said, with a sudden flash of inspiration. 'There's a locker full of clean towels. Any good?'

Claude thought about this. It wasn't ideal but it would have to do. Richie went back to the boat and returned with two large blue towels. He and Claude stood over the severed head, sizing up the task.

'Well, let's not make it any more complicated than it needs to be,' said Claude.

He got Richie to open out one of the towels and hold it outstretched with both arms. He took the other towel in his hands and waited a moment for the waves to recede, leaving the head temporarily stationary on the sand. Then he bent down and picked it up quickly and cleanly. He placed it in the middle of Richie's towel and together they managed to wrap it up completely.

It looked like a big blue ball. Or a macabre version of a big blue ball.

They set off back to the hotel with Richie driving the boat as slowly as he could. Claude sat holding the head with Marjorie perched next to him. Strangely, now that the offending object was wrapped up and out of sight, she professed herself to be feeling a little better.

'What are we going to do with it?' she asked.

Claude had already been musing on this. It would probably be some time before the police arrived and it was still an extremely hot day. He had considered using one of the hotel's fridges or freezers temporarily but in the end ruled it out because it would only have introduced more contamination into the equation. He realised there was nothing for it but to simply carry on holding the head himself.

'Does your little office at Watersports have air conditioning?' he asked Richie.

Richie confirmed that it did.

'Right. That's where we're going.'

They eventually made it back to Circular Island and Richie beached the boat. Fortunately there seemed to be no-one around except Kath. Richie briefed her as they walked up the beach and she listened, wide-eyed. She agreed to guard the door as they reached the office and the other three went inside. Richie turned the air conditioning down as far as it would go and Claude sat himself down, still holding the dreaded parcel. He asked Richie to ring the manager and put the phone on speaker. It rang several times.

'Michael Hayden.'

Claude leant forward towards the phone.

'Ah Mr Hayden, it's Claude Simmons. I'm afraid we have some bad news for you. There's no easy way to put this but . . . we've found a severed head at Oblong Island.'

Mr Hayden had evidently also been on speakerphone because there was the distinct sound of the receiver suddenly being picked up.

'And is it Mr Anderson?'

Under the circumstances, Marjorie thought this was a ridiculous question.

'It's difficult to tell,' she said. 'He's not really looking himself at the moment.'

She was definitely back to normal.

'Look Mr Hayden, you're going to have to do a couple more things I'm afraid,' said Claude, ignoring Marjorie. 'Contact the police again. They need to send more troops. And they need a full forensic team. Also, you're going to have to stop anyone leaving the island.'

'But Mr and Mrs Gough are checking out as we speak. They're headed back to Brisbane.'

'Not for the time being they're not.'

There was a prolonged silence.

'What . . . are you saying it's murder?'

Claude thought about this, still clutching the severed head.

'Too soon to tell.'

Richie went off to see how Kath was coping. This left Claude and Marjorie sitting in silence for a while.

'Actually, I'm a bit lost,' Marjorie said eventually.

Claude looked at her. This was her frequent lament.

'I mean, the nasty big sharks are out in the deep water beyond the reef, according to Richie. And for Don Anderson to get to them he would have had to have swum across about thirty yards of sharp pointy coral, probably in the dark. How does that work?'

She thought about this for a moment longer.

'And if someone else had attacked him and then wanted to feed him to the sharks, that person would have had to have swum out over the coral, dragging his body along at the same time. Even more ridiculous.'

Claude pondered this. Actually, Marjorie wasn't lost. She was making some extremely good observations.

CHAPTER TWELVE

The seaplane landed just as the sun was setting. Richie had been waiting in the speedboat and drove out to meet it. He helped to tie the plane up to a buoy in the deeper water beyond the reef and four passengers clambered out. They jumped down into the boat, bringing with them a small amount of luggage and a considerable number of serious looking metal cases.

'Looks like the cavalry's arrived,' said Marjorie. She and Claude were standing on the beach watching proceedings, along with most of the hotel's other guests. Two other police officers - Sergeant Wilkes and Constable Chappell - had arrived earlier, by boat from Cairns. They had finally relieved Claude of the severed head and placed it in a large evidence bag. They had also bagged up both of the towels that had been used in the retrieval process.

The newcomers made their way up the beach towards the hotel, guided by Richie. Three of them struggled with their metal cases while the fourth strode on ahead. He had a certain air of authority about him and looked as if he might be in charge. He surveyed the small crowd as he walked past and his gaze seemed to settle on Claude and Marjorie for a moment.

The crowd dispersed and most people found their way to the bar for a drink and a good gossip. Inevitably, word had gone round about the severed head and Claude and Marjorie's role in discovering it. When they themselves arrived at the bar they were inundated with questions from guests who professed to be horrified about the incident whilst at the same time probing for every last gory detail. Frank Gough seemed downright annoyed that his travel plans had been disrupted.

Claude did his best to keep everyone at bay while Marjorie ordered them each a drink. They took the drinks and found a table as far away from the commotion as they could. They sat sipping their drinks, discussing the tumultuous day and what lay ahead. They hadn't got very far when Constable Chappell arrived at their table.

'Mr Simmons, Mrs Watson. I wonder if you could spare a moment for the Superintendent please?'

This sounded ominous. They followed the Constable into the hotel and he led them to a room which the police had clearly requisitioned as some sort of nerve centre. Sergeant Wilkes was working at a white board writing up what little information the police currently had, beneath a picture of Don Anderson. In the middle of the room stood the man who had caught their gaze earlier. He was probably in his forties and, although not in uniform, was nonetheless quite smartly dressed.

'Good evening. I'm Superintendent Bill Niles of the Queensland Police Service. I am now the officer in charge of this investigation.'

Marjorie attempted to introduce herself and Claude but the Superintendent interrupted her.

'I know who you are,' he said, a little rudely Marjorie thought.

'You're the ones who discovered the victim and decided to remove the remains from the scene.'

'But...' said Marjorie, anxiously.

The Superintendent raised his hand.

'And you've been giving quite a lot of orders, apparently. Sealing off rooms. Banning everyone from leaving the island.'

He began to pace around, seeming to weigh up the charges. He stopped again in front of Claude and Marjorie. He looked at them both.

'We're very grateful. It looks like you've helped us

avoid a whole lot of problems.'

Claude and Marjorie glanced at each other. They were both surprised.

'Having said that, you can leave everything to us now,' the Superintendent continued, sounding as if he was trying to be helpful. 'I suggest you try and relax and enjoy the rest of your holiday. Now if you'll excuse us, we have a great deal of forensic work to be getting on with.'

Marjorie took the news badly. 'So what you're saying is: "Well done and now bugger off"?'

It was the Superintendent's turn to look surprised. Claude quickly intervened. In any event he wasn't feeling he was quite ready to bugger off.

'Sorry Superintendent, but there's actually one more thing anyway.'

He explained about Mrs Anderson and her bizarre behaviour at the pool earlier that morning.

'The manager is going to tell you that she was still drunk from the night before. I'm going to tell you that she may well have been drugged. Probably worth a blood test, while you're collecting all your forensic evidence.'

With that, he and Marjorie turned and walked back out of the door.

The Superintendent was left staring at Sergeant

Wilkes. The Sergeant shrugged.

Claude and Marjorie set off to return to their rooms. When they arrived they found that the door to the Anderson's neighbouring hut was now wide open. It was being carefully examined by a forensic technician in full protective clothing. They wandered round to get a better view and joined the small crowd of guests that had gathered again. Inside, they could see a second technician, working with what appeared to be an ultraviolet light.

Constable Chappell arrived to disperse the crowd and Claude and Marjorie went off to change for dinner. They met up again and headed for the restaurant. They were greeted even more enthusiastically by the other guests than they had been at the pool bar earlier. There were a number of smiling "Good evenings" and even several attempts at handshakes as they walked through to their table. It was as if they now had some sort of celebrity status. The reason became obvious when Shane appeared at the table. He was grinning.

'So, it turns out you're those two doddery detectives who solved the murder at The Farm?'

He had meant this as a compliment but had somehow badly mangled it along the way. Marjorie glared at him.

'Who told you that?'

He looked a bit panicky. It was clearly either Michael Hayden or Richie who had told him but he didn't want to drop either of them in it. He gestured to the other guests in the restaurant, grinning again.

'Everyone's talking about it.'

As if to underline the point, Barry arrived, cradling an expensive looking bottle of wine. Barry tended to double up as wine waiter during the evenings.

'Good evening. This is our best bottle and it comes with the compliments of the couple at table eight.'

Claude and Marjorie looked across at table eight. It was Ian and Dawn from Melbourne. They seemed to have conveniently forgotten Marjorie's yarn about her and Claude's diamond wedding anniversary and now had their glasses raised in salutation. Claude raised his glass in return and smiled. Marjorie gave them a regal wave.

'I feel that our audience is demanding an encore,' she said.

◆ ◆ ◆

By the time they set off for breakfast the next morning, the police team had already been extremely busy. To begin with, the seaplane had left at first light. It contained one of the forensic technicians and all of the forensic evidence they had so far been able to gather, including the severed head. They were on their way back to Cairns and the pathology lab.

A second forensic technician had seconded Richie and the game fishing boat and they were halfway to Oblong Island. The Superintendent had stipulated that the island needed to be searched thoroughly. And that an extensive sweep needed to be made of the surrounding waters.

The final technician was also hard at work. He had erected a tent on the sand some way off and appeared to be busy inside. Claude paused and surveyed the scene. He was impressed with the team's thoroughness.

'I feel like everyone's busy except us,' said Marjorie as they sat down for breakfast. This was a worrying sign. Shane arrived and they both ordered bacon and egg with fried tomato. Claude looked out of the window for a moment.

'There's not much we can do right now anyway,' he said. 'The path lab has still got the unenviable task of trying to establish the cause of death. Don't forget there's still the distinct possibility that this is simply death by misadventure.'

She almost looked disappointed. She wanted to know if Claude really thought that might be a possibility.

Claude paused. He had no intention of pouring petrol on Marjorie's flames.

'In all my years in the Met I never saw anything quite so badly mutilated. I really have no idea.'

They finished their breakfast and made their way to the pool. They ordered a coffee from the bar and took up residence on two loungers. Claude opened his Bradman biography, intent on finishing the final chapter. He settled back, doing his best to transmit a "Do Not Disturb" signal. Marjorie picked up her cosy murder mystery. To be honest, she was still in an irritable mood and she was starting to struggle with the book, what with all the red herrings and the blind alleys. It was nothing like a real murder, she thought to herself.

In any case, she was constantly being interrupted by other guests. She put her book down and looked around. A strange thing seemed to have happened. Alyssa's lounger was no longer the most popular place at the pool. Marjorie's was.

'Lovely day isn't it? Any news?'

'What a pretty top. Have they arrested anyone yet?'

'How well you're looking. Is it true they've found another body part?'

She was positively inundated with questions from seemingly casual passers-by. She was in the process of letting this go to her head when Sergeant Wilkes arrived with another question.

'Mrs Watson, Mr Simmons. Could we take your witness statement now please?'

They followed him back into the hotel, to another room that had been requisitioned. It was starting to look like the police were taking over the whole resort. They all sat down and the Sergeant produced a pad and pen.

'Perhaps we could start with the discovery of the remains at Oblong Island?'

Marjorie didn't have much to contribute to this and Claude set off on a long and detailed description of events. Sergeant Wilkes wrote all of it down even though, in truth, it wasn't really anything the police hadn't already worked out. He looked up at Claude.

'But why did you make the journey to the island in the first place?'

Claude was about to explain himself, including his experiences as a child in Cornwall. However, Marjorie felt a contribution coming on, offended by the slight note of suspicion in the question.

'Because he used to be a Detective Chief Superintendent,' she said, laying particular emphasis on the word "Chief". 'He's clever like that.'

Sergeant Wilkes blinked back at her. He felt he had little choice but to dutifully write down "Detective

Chief Superintendent".

'There's one more thing,' said Claude. 'On our first night here, Marjorie and I overheard an argument between a man and a woman down at the water's edge.'

'What sort of argument?' asked the Sergeant, now extremely interested.

Claude recounted what they'd been able to see and hear that night, particularly emphasising the slightly physical nature of the exchange.

'The point is, we're absolutely certain the man was Don Anderson.'

'Went back into hut number six,' Marjorie added.

The Sergeant looked up.

'And the woman? She was his wife?'

Claude shook his head. 'Sorry, she went off in the other direction. We have no idea.'

They finished their statement and got up to leave.

'By the way, how is Mrs Anderson?' asked Marjorie.

'Oh, much better physically. But as you'd expect, she's very shaken up.'

'And has she had anything to say about last night?' asked Claude, fishing for information.

Sergeant Wilkes had been ready for that one.

'She's giving her statement to the Superintendent now. So we don't really know yet.'

◆ ◆ ◆

The seaplane landed again at about five in the afternoon. Richie was waiting in the speedboat with one of the forensic team. The door of the plane was opened and a metal case containing the day's forensic evidence was loaded on board. A document bag was handed back out in exchange. The door was closed and the plane took off again. Richie drove the speedboat back to the beach and his passenger ran off towards the hotel.

Superintendent Niles had already spoken to the pathologist by phone and knew the result of the preliminary autopsy. Nonetheless, he was keen to read the written report in its entirety. He reached into the document bag and pulled out the first of two folders. He opened it and took his time reading the contents. He pulled out the second folder and did the same. He sat back in his chair and gazed out of the window, collecting his thoughts.

'Right, Constable Chappell. We need everyone assembled at the pool in fifteen minutes please. Guests, staff, the lot. Sergeant Wilkes, you need to speak to Mrs Anderson.'

The two officers exited in different directions. Constable Chappell set to work and eventually succeeded in rounding up the island's one hundred or so residents, minus Mrs Anderson. They milled around expectantly at the pool, speculating noisily about what the announcement might be.

The Superintendent emerged from inside the hotel and everyone fell silent. He stood in front of them and briefly introduced himself. The crowd leaned forward anxiously for the news. It was brief and straight to the point.

'I am sorry to tell you that the initial pathology report confirms that Don Anderson was indeed murdered.'

There were gasps of astonishment. Claude and Marjorie stood at the back of the crowd, watching the shocked reactions.

'Please! Please!' called out the Superintendent, trying to make himself heard above the hubbub.

Eventually the crowd fell silent again.

'Unfortunately, that means that Circular Island is now officially a crime scene and current restrictions will have to continue. Please contact your family, your friends, your place of work - everyone will be staying here for the time being.'

There were groans from a number of guests and a loud 'bloody hell!' from Frank Gough.

'Since this is now a murder inquiry, we will be asking the hotel for the basic information you all gave when you registered here – address, email address, mobile phone number. If anyone has a problem with that, please come and see me. In the meantime, we will do our best to keep you informed. Thank you.'

The Superintendent turned and walked back into the hotel, ignoring the rising crescendo of questions behind him.

He returned to his chair in the investigation room and put his feet up on the desk. He had some thinking to do. He was an extremely capable police officer and had risen to the rank of Superintendent early in his career, after a number of successful cases. But now he was in a difficult situation. He was responsible for solving a grisly, high-profile murder whilst at the same time holding a large group of people captive. And most of those people were rich and entirely capable of voicing a sense of entitlement extremely loudly. He had already watched their fascination with the murder turn into frustration at their enforced confinement. He knew the situation could easily spill over into complete insurrection.

But he was smart and savvy and he was entirely capable of being unorthodox if the situation required. He had absolutely no interest in throwing his rank around or in jealously guarding his territory. And he had absolutely no interest in following the rules if it was going to get him nowhere. Weighing the situation up logically he came to the only possible conclusion. He needed more help.

He reached forward and picked up the phone.

◆ ◆ ◆

Claude and Marjorie arrived for dinner as usual. They were greeted by Shane who looked even more enthusiastic than normal.

'Good evening! I've put you on a special table this evening, right out of the way. You know, to stop everybody earwigging your conversation.'

Marjorie looked at Claude. What on earth was he talking about?

They followed Shane to a table right at the edge of the dining area, half hidden behind a large hibiscus, replete with bright red flowers. Already seated at the table was Superintendent Niles.

'Good evening,' he said, standing up. 'I was rather hoping you might join me for dinner.'

Claude and Marjorie were surprised but nonetheless delighted. Everyone sat down. They all studied their menus and quickly got their food and drink orders out of the way. Shane set off for the kitchen, smiling broadly. He was delighted to be involved in whatever subterfuge it was that was taking place.

Claude and Marjorie looked at the Superintendent, waiting for him to explain himself. Was it subterfuge? Or were they in trouble again?

He took a moment to collect his thoughts.

'Look, I'm not an idiot.'

He paused. Marjorie thought about responding but, on balance, felt she didn't know him well enough to comment one way or the other.

'Obviously, I know about your involvement in the Stephen Kenny case. And in the business with Gregg Perry.'

He paused again.

'Very impressive.'

Marjorie was pleased. A compliment. Superintendent Niles was definitely not an idiot.

'My colleagues in the Northern Territories Police tell me you have Special Adviser status with the UK police. So I've taken the liberty of asking the opinion of your commanding officer about involving you in this case...'

He produced his notebook from the inside pocket of his linen jacket and opened it.

'... Chief Constable Selby is it? He had some very specific advice for me.'

He flicked past a couple of pages in the notebook

and began reading.

'Ah yes . . . "You have two choices. Side line them and you'll find yourself undermined, double-crossed and most likely humiliated. And that's just Marjorie Watson".'

The Superintendent looked at Marjorie.

'I assume he's referring to the fact that you tried to hire a contract killer in Brisbane?'

'Well, amongst other things, yes,' Marjorie replied. She was delighted. She felt the compliments were now coming thick and fast.

He referred back to his notebook again.

' " . . . or invite them to join the investigation. Might still be a bit bumpy but you'll almost certainly get a result".'

He closed his notebook and put it back in his pocket. He looked at them both.

'I've decided to opt for the latter, if it's okay with you.'

Marjorie and Claude glanced at each other. This was excellent news.

The Superintendent briefly outlined the rules of engagement for the new enterprise: Queensland Police to be in charge at all times; the Superintendent himself to approve all investigative decisions; Claude and Marjorie to act only as informal observers and advisers.

They were pleased to accept. This time, Marjorie was definitely going to follow the rules.

'Can I ask?' said Claude. 'Why the change of heart, Superintendent?'

Shane had brought the drinks for everybody. The Superintendent took a sip of his red wine, composing his thoughts.

'Oh, you know. I had a long philosophical debate with myself and I agonised about it for hours and hours. Then the results of the drug test for Lynne Anderson came back from the path lab.' He smiled, clearly mocking himself. 'You were right again Mr Simmons. She was positive for Phenobarbital.'

Marjorie clapped Claude on the back, even though she had no real idea what phenobarbital was. Claude was glad to have been proven right. But his detective's instincts had already moved on to the next question.

'And what about Don Anderson? Were they able to tell if he'd been drugged as well?'

'They were. He had.'

CHAPTER THIRTEEN

'It's a barbiturate usually used for treating epilepsy. But its major side-effect is drowsiness. In large doses, it can even produce coma.'

They were at breakfast the following morning and Claude was trying to explain the properties of Phenobarbital to Marjorie. He had seen it used a number of times in his career, almost always by someone trying to subdue a prospective victim.

Marjorie was listening intently, demolishing a pair of poached eggs at the same time.

'So, since they were both drugged, we can assume Lynne Anderson is innocent, can't we?'

Claude looked up from his bacon omelette. He tried to phrase his answer as diplomatically as he could.

'Yes . . . except . . . what if she drugged her husband before attacking him and then self-administered her own dose of phenobarbital afterwards. You know, to make herself look innocent?'

'Bugger,' said Marjorie. She didn't feel she was at the top of her game.

They finished breakfast and went back into the main part of the hotel. They had been invited to the morning police briefing at ten o'clock and made their way to the investigation room. Sergeant Wilkes and Constable Chappell stood chatting with the three forensic technicians and Claude and Marjorie found themselves two seats at the back of the room. They sat down and squinted at the investigation board. It contained considerably more information than when they had first seen it, now including a picture of Lynne Anderson, beneath that of her husband.

Superintendent Niles entered the room and all the others sat down.

'Just to confirm,' he said. 'The purpose of these meetings is for all of us to brief each other on every single piece of evidence or information that is discovered. So speak up if you have something to say.'

Everybody nodded.

The Superintendent opened the folder he carried with him and took out a series of photographs of the severed head, including several close-ups. It was a gruesome start. He stuck them to the board and Marjorie was forced to look away for a second.

'The pathologist has concluded that the victim was struck a number of times, almost certainly before he entered the water.'

He pointed to one of the close-ups which showed what appeared to be a mass of livid and ugly bruising and several contusions on the victim's right temple.

'In any event, the wounds were definitely not caused by impact with coral or rocks but by a series of blows from a small, flat object. Most probably the head of a hammer.'

This caused a slight stir in the room. Sergeant Wilkes had a question.

'And was he dead before he went into the water, sir?'

The Superintendent thought about this for a second.

'The pathologist can't be certain but I don't think it matters very much. I doubt the murderer cared one way or the other and a tiger shark certainly wouldn't have been bothered. My working premise is that, whoever the murderer was, he or she was trying to achieve three simple things: immobilise Don Anderson completely; make sure there was plenty of blood; somehow get his body out into the deeper water beyond the reef. After that, the sharks were supposed to do the rest and neatly dispose of all the evidence. The bite marks around the victim's neck show that the plan very nearly succeeded.'

Claude sat listening attentively to all of this. He thought it was an excellent hypothesis.

The Superintendent added two more things: the pathologist estimated the time of death as anywhere between 1am and 6am and could be no more precise; blood and tissue analysis indicated the amount of phenobarbital administered to Don and Lynne Anderson had been considerable.

The Superintendent sat down and the lead forensic technician took his place in front of the white board. He read from his notes with an update. First of all, the search of Oblong Island and the surrounding waters had produced nothing. Some samples had been brought back but none of them proved to be human remains. The Anderson's hut had been equally unproductive. There was no blood, no signs of a struggle and no significant fingerprints, once those of the cleaners and waiting staff had been eliminated. Tellingly, no phenobarbital was discovered either. However, traces of blood had been found in several places on the beach. The pathology lab had rung that morning to confirm that the blood was that of Don Anderson.

The forensic technician sat back down and Sergeant Wilkes took his place. He was, he said, continuing to take witness statements from the Island's residents and had so far interviewed 14 couples and 16 members of staff. He shared Claude and Marjorie's statement with everybody, with particular reference to the argument at the shoreline. However, apart from that he had gathered little else that he thought was useful. There was a great deal of speculation, rumour and even a few wild accusations among the interviewees, he said. But given that the murder had taken place in the middle of the night, nobody had actually seen or heard anything.

Finally, it was Constable Chappell's turn. He was liaising with a small group of police officers back at the police station in Cairns who were involved in digital forensics. They were in the process of retrieving Don Anderson's phone and computer data and attempting to cross-match it with the basic data for staff and guests, provided by the hotel.

Claude continued to look on from the side lines. He suddenly realised that he'd missed something out from his and Marjorie's earlier witness statement. He put his hand up.

'Sorry. There's something I should have told Sergeant Wilkes earlier. Frank Gough and Don Anderson knew each other. They fell out about the purchase of a speedboat, apparently.'

The Constable was pleased to make a note in his notebook. It was a small lead, but a lead nonetheless.

The Superintendent stood up again, looking as if he was ready to leave.

'Good,' he said. 'Given that we now have at least some significant forensic evidence, I'd like to try and carry out a reconstruction of the crime. See if we can get a few things straight in our minds about what's happened here. Shall we meet again in an hour?'

The Superintendent and his team set off, leaving Claude and Marjorie to weigh up what they'd just seen and heard. Marjorie was struggling a little. Apart from anything else, there seemed so much information to process. She looked at Claude for guidance.

He shrugged. 'Extremely efficient, I thought.'

He got up and walked to the investigation board. Actually, there were a few details he still wanted to know about the case. He scanned the Post-It notes and the magic marker scrawls and eventually found the two facts he was looking for. There was a third piece of information as well.

'Crikey, he was only thirty one,' said Claude, pointing at the board.

'Why "crikey"?'

"Well, it's a bit young to be the sales director of a fairly major corporation, isn't it?'

Marjorie thought about this.

'Probably not, if your dad's the boss.'

◆ ◆ ◆

The team crammed themselves into the Anderson's hut. All eyes were on Superintendent Niles.

'I think we should probably start with Lynne Anderson's alibi,' he said. 'See if we think it stands up to scrutiny.'

Her statement, he explained, said that she and her husband had returned from dinner on the night in question, both feeling extremely groggy. She claimed they ate and drank normally and the restaurant confirmed they each had two courses and shared a single bottle of wine. They finished the evening with coffee at the poolside bar. Nonetheless, they could barely make their way back to the hut. They apparently managed to struggle their way into bed and Mrs Anderson claimed to remember nothing more until morning.

Sergeant Wilkes looked a little daunted at the work that was coming his way. He knew that Mrs Anderson could have administered both doses of Phenobarbital. But at this moment it could also have been any one of a number of kitchen, waiting and bar staff. He had a lot more interviewing to do.

The Superintendent walked back outside the hut and everyone followed. He looked back at the open door before continuing.

'There were no signs of forced entry. So, if her story is true, it suggests that someone may have entered the room with a pass key.'

'Or perhaps the door was never locked,' said Marjorie, trying to make a contribution. 'I haven't been locking my door. Didn't seem much point on a desert island. Well, not until someone got murdered.'

Everybody looked at her.

'Anyway, they were both drugged up to the eyeballs when they came back from the bar. They probably left the door wide open.'

The Superintendent thought about this. Actually, he couldn't really disagree.

'In any event,' he continued, turning away from the door and setting off towards a palm tree some way off, 'our working theory says he was either dragged from his bed or somehow persuaded to stumble as far as here.'

He stopped on the other side of the palm tree. It was one of a row that marked the end of the accommodation area and the beginning of the beach. This was where Claude and Marjorie had seen the forensic technician working inside his tent. The area still had a small cordon of tape around it.

'We believe that this is where Mr Anderson was attacked.'

The forensic technician in question stepped forward and explained that a large amount of Don Anderson's blood had been successfully reclaimed from the sand. Claude looked impressed. He wasn't sure that such a forensic process was even possible in his day.

The Superintendent walked on to another cordoned-off area.

'More blood here.'

And then on to another.

'And here.'

The three areas formed a very obvious straight line and the Superintendent set off in the direction to which the line pointed.

'By this time, we are assuming Mr Anderson was unconscious and therefore being dragged. The destination seems to have been Watersports.'

Everybody dutifully followed behind. Marjorie looked over to the "Do Not Cross" tape that Sergeant Wilkes and Constable Chappell had put up some way off. A large number of hotel guests were pressed up against it, eagerly trying to determine what was going on.

The Superintendent reached the water's edge and turned back to face the others.

'Round about here, everything gets a bit hazy. Having dragged the body this far, how did the murderer then tow it right out to the deep water? In the dark and across an extremely large coral reef?'

Up to now, Claude had been listening intently and deliberately keeping quiet. However, he assumed that the Superintendent was now inviting opinions.

'Marjorie and I have been debating this. We're not sure it's even possible.'

Sergeant Wilkes stepped forward.

'I've checked with Richie Gilmour, the head of Watersports, sir.' He opened his notebook. 'He says it would be very difficult, even for a strong swimmer. It would almost certainly result in severe cuts and abrasions and considerable loss of blood.'

'Which means you could be trying to murder someone and easily end up feeding yourself to the sharks,' said Marjorie, putting a neat full stop on the end of the argument.

Everybody looked temporarily stumped. They walked slowly around the Watersports area, searching for ideas. A thought seemed to occur to Claude and the Superintendent at exactly the same time. They both walked towards a brightly coloured group of four kayaks and three canoes, pulled up together on the beach. They looked at the boats and then they looked at each other.

'Have these been given the forensic once-over?' asked the Superintendent, turning to the forensic technicians and pointing to the boats.

They all shook their heads.

'Well, perhaps we should do it now?'

There was a flurry of activity. One of the technicians ran off to get their protective clothing and they eventually suited up and started carrying the boats one by one back towards the hotel.

The Superintendent set off with Claude and Marjorie to slowly walk the crime scene again, this time in reverse.

'So, what do you think of Mrs Anderson's alibi?' asked the Superintendent, after a while.

Claude collected his thoughts. 'Honestly, I don't think I'm any the wiser about her alibi. But I think the big thing that's emerged from the reconstruction is that she absolutely couldn't have carried out the murder on her own. She had to have had an accomplice.'

The Superintendent shrugged. He had come to the same conclusion.

'I mean, according to your investigation board Don Anderson weighed over fourteen stone,' Claude continued.

'I know. And he was six foot two.'

Marjorie was following on behind, not able to make a contribution. Actually, she was starting to feel irritated with what she saw as the love-in that was developing between Claude and the Superintendent.

'And what does Mrs Anderson weigh?' Claude asked.

'Eight stone, wringing wet,' said Marjorie, jumping in quickly.

They had reached the area where the blood had been found in the sand and they stopped for a moment.

'Exactly,' said Claude. 'And how does an eight stone woman drag a fourteen stone man seventy or eighty yards? And then possibly heave him into a canoe? And then heave the canoe into the water?'

The Superintendent had got the point.

'Let's agree,' he said, wearily. 'We're looking for two murderers.'

CHAPTER FOURTEEN

'But why am I having to talk to you two as well?'

Lynne Anderson was bemoaning her lot. It was mid-morning and she was sat with Claude and Marjorie in the otherwise deserted breakfast room. The Superintendent had allowed the meeting to take place, on the strict understanding that the murder itself wasn't discussed in any way. The conversation had been underway for about ten minutes and was extremely heavy going.

'Well, umm,' said Claude, trying again. 'All we'd really like to know is just a little more about your husband, if that's okay.'

'What for? So you can gossip with the other guests?'

She looked strained and her eyes were red-rimmed and puffy.

'Actually, we've been assisting the Queensland police' said Marjorie. 'The Superintendent himself asked if we could help out.'

Mrs Anderson looked baffled as to why two eighty

year olds should be working for the police. Since her husband's murder she had taken refuge inside the new room she'd been given by the manager and she'd heard none of the stories about Claude and Marjorie's exploits.

'Look, we don't need to do this if you're unhappy about it Mrs Anderson,' said Claude, trying once more. 'But we'd just like to hear about your husband's background. You know, his achievements, his career, his life with you. We're only trying to help.'

She thought about it for what seemed an age, toying absently with her coffee cup. Her mood seemed to soften.

'Actually, people always think Don got the job at CobaltBlue because of his father.'

Claude looked at Marjorie.

'But the truth is, he was a natural-born salesman. Could charm the birds out of the trees if he wanted to.'

'So he was successful?' asked Claude.

'Just a bit. Doubled the company's order book in three years.'

She seemed genuinely proud of her husband. She went on to explain that he had toured the country tirelessly as CobaltBlue's representative. While their family home was in Brisbane, he selflessly spent a large part of his time at the other famous sailing centres in Australia – Sydney, Hobart in Tasmania and Fremantle in Western Australia. Just before they'd arrived at The Island Hotel he'd apparently sold two big boats in Fremantle.

'Some weeks I hardly even saw him.' She smiled briefly. She obviously meant this as a compliment to her husband and his boundless industry and perhaps as a testament to the strength of their marriage. Nonetheless, it sounded slightly strange to Claude and Marjorie.

She paused for a moment, lost in her memories.

'Do you have any children?' asked Marjorie.

Mrs Anderson returned to toying with her coffee cup.

'No we don't,' she said, still clearly keen to describe herself and her husband as "we". She looked back at Claude and Marjorie, suddenly slightly tearful. 'Don was keen to start a family but I wanted to wait until I'd turned thirty. I mean, it felt like we were on top of the world and I wanted to enjoy it while I could. Stupid, selfish bitch.' She reached into her bag for a tissue.

Claude and Marjorie tried several more questions but the moment had passed. Eventually Mrs Anderson got up, blubbered an apology and headed back to her room.

Claude looked at Marjorie. He knew there was a

question coming and he sat patiently waiting for it.

'Do you think she did it?'

Claude had rashly predicted the outcome of a murder enquiry when he was a young detective and had made a fool of himself in front of his commanding officer. He had never forgotten the experience and never made the same mistake again. That didn't mean he didn't have a view on Marjorie's question and, in actual fact, he thought it was extremely unlikely that Mrs Anderson was involved in the murder. He just wasn't going to come out and say it.

'Much too soon to tell Marjorie. There are still an awful lot of questions to be answered.' Actually, Claude wasn't just keeping his own counsel. He quite enjoyed this little game.

She looked at him, frustrated. She got up from the table.

'Our next appointment is in an hour,' she said, rather officiously. 'Shall we sit by the pool?'

They left the breakfast room and found two loungers near the bar. It was a bit too early for a gin and tonic, even for Marjorie, and they settled in for a brief bit of people watching.

The deterioration in mood among the hotel's guests was palpable. Nobody seemed to be doing any lounging. There was hardly anyone in the pool. Scarcely a book had been picked up. Instead, everybody sat bolt upright, each scanning their fellow guests nervously. A cloud of suspicion seemed to have temporarily blocked out the tropical sunshine.

Alyssa sat alone, her long line of suitors having now entirely disappeared. It was as if the grimness of the murder had at least restored some sense of propriety among the island's male population, Marjorie thought. Even Barry the barman was giving her a wide berth.

Inside the investigation room they took up their normal seats at the back. The rest of the team assembled and the lead forensic technician stood up to speak. As ever, he got straight to the point.

'Close examination of the boats yesterday revealed numerous traces of blood on one of the canoes.'

He produced a photograph from the folder in front of him and stuck it on the investigation board. It showed a bright red canoe, littered with numbered stickers that presumably indicated the areas where the blood was found.

'Overnight tests at the lab in Cairns have determined that the blood was that of Don Anderson.'

This produced a brief murmur.

'And fingerprints?' asked the Superintendent.

'Unfortunately, lots of them. Watersports estimate

the canoes are taken out by guests at least three or four times a day. Often used by the staff as well. We're going to end up trying to rule out half of the island.'

One step forwards and one step sideways, thought Claude. Unfortunately, there were also a number of other sideways steps still to come.

Sergeant Wilkes stood up and announced that he had finished interviewing the staff and the guests. No useful evidence had been forthcoming. He was now re-interviewing staff members with regard to the administering of the phenobarbital. Again, there were a number of allegations and accusations from the interviewees about each other but no reliable evidence as yet. In what sounded like an attempt to justify the lack of progress, he reported that the preparation of one plate of food could easily involve four kitchen staff and two waiting staff. The Superintendent looked unimpressed.

Constable Chappell was next. Apparently Mrs Anderson had agreed to hand over her phone and had allowed access to her computer and iPad. The digital team in Cairns were now analysing the data in an attempt to find possible links to an accomplice. In the meantime, all attempts to cross-match Don Anderson's data with the phone numbers and email addresses of staff and guests had been fruitless, aside from one email from Frank Gough about the purchase of a speedboat. There appeared to be no other contact with anyone on the island.

Superintendent Niles stood up, clearly frustrated.

'And what about the weapon that the victim was attacked with?' he asked, hoping for a little forward momentum.

'Sorry sir, work in progress,' said the lead technician. 'We've recovered three hammers - two from the hotel's maintenance department and one from the gardeners. So far we've failed to find any traces of blood or tissue. They've gone back to Cairns for further analysis.'

'Right,' said the Superintendent, frowning. 'Let's keep at it. Any questions?'

Claude put his hand up. He had no desire to further demoralise the Superintendent but he had a question nonetheless.

'I know the circumstances possibly point to Mrs Anderson at the moment, but what are we suggesting her motive might be? Is there a large amount of money in Don Anderson's name? Or a big insurance policy?'

The Superintendent's frown deepened. He looked to Sergeant Wilkes, hoping for moral support. Unfortunately, there wasn't any.

'Brisbane police have been investigating the couple's

background. There is a life insurance policy – related to Mr Anderson's employment at CobaltBlue – but it isn't huge. However, the Brisbane police describe their lifestyle as . . .' He read from his notes. '. . . "quite extravagant". There seem to be no savings to speak of. There is a large house but there's also a large mortgage attached to it.'

Superintendent Niles looked at Claude and shrugged There was clearly a long way to go.

◆ ◆ ◆

There was little further progress over the next few days. The three hammers came back from the lab but none of them had tested positive for any kind of genetic material. Added to that, the pathologist considered that they were all too large for the wounds that Don Anderson had sustained.

Forensics had ground to a halt. Digital forensics had ground to a halt. Sergeant Wilkes had now interviewed all of the staff for a second time about the administering of the phenobarbital and drawn a complete blank.

Understandably, the guests were growing extremely restless. Requests to leave the island were becoming louder and more persistent by the day. The more resourceful among the guests had also recruited their lawyers to join in with the lobbying. There were dark mutterings about "unlawful detainment" and "false imprisonment".

Then there was the manager. He was being forced to turn away new guests on a daily basis and his complaints to the Superintendent were becoming incessant.

Worst of all, Marjorie was starting to become uppity.

'I really think we should be digging into people's backgrounds a bit more,' she said, interrupting yet another briefing session. She hadn't even bothered to put her hand up. 'Why don't we start with this Alyssa woman? There's something very odd about her.'

This stopped everyone short. Sergeant Wilkes looked at his notes.

'Alyssa Brown. 26. From Perth.' He was trying to seem efficient.

'Yes I'm sure she is,' said Marjorie, dismissively. 'But the point is, what's she doing here? And on her own? Does anyone really believe this story about the modelling assignment?'

'Oh, I definitely believe it,' said the Superintendent, stepping in to try and quickly quash the rebellion. 'But then I've had the swimwear company she was working for on the phone twice, threatening to take me to court.'

He looked less than pleased. This didn't deter Marjorie.

'And what about her fiancé? Where's he gone to?'

The Superintendent looked at his two officers. Had they all missed something?

'Sorry, are you saying he's been here? On the island?'

'No, no, no, that's the whole point. He hasn't been here. Why not?'

Now even Claude was confused.

The Superintendent looked at Marjorie, narrowing his eyes. He spelled out that there were currently no grounds for investigating Alyssa Brown further. In any event, to do so would probably mean having to arrest her.

'And on what grounds would you like us to do that, Mrs Watson?' He allowed himself to lapse into sarcasm. 'Failing to have a fiancé?'

The meeting ended and Claude steered Marjorie out of the investigation room.

'Stupid bloody man,' she said.

He wasn't entirely sure where her outburst had come from and knew it was pointless to ask. They found a table by the bar and Claude ordered her a Marjorita, in the spirit of being supportive. It eventually arrived and she sat sipping it, pensively.

'I know I don't have a lot of evidence but I'm absolutely certain she's involved in it somehow. I'd bet all of my Stephen Kenny reward money on it.'

'Claude saw an opportunity to lighten the mood.

'Well you don't need to do that Marjorie. How about instead I offer you double or nothing on the dollar bet we already have? You say she's guilty and, for the sake of sportsmanship, I'll say she's innocent.'

It wasn't clear if Marjorie fully understood the significance of this offer. Nonetheless, she held out her hand towards Claude, keen to demonstrate how confident she was in her theory.

'Deal.'

◆ ◆ ◆

There was a loud knock at Claude's door. It was seven thirty in the morning and he had almost finished getting dressed. He walked to the door, fastening the last button on his linen shirt. Outside was Sergeant Wilkes. He was out of breath.

'One of the hotel's boats is missing. Everyone's gathering at Watersports in five minutes.'

He dashed off again, presumably to alert another member of the team.

Claude walked across to Marjorie's hut to see if she was awake yet. She wasn't. He continued to knock and eventually she peered round the door, looking a little bleary eyed. Possibly the final Marjorita had been a mistake. He explained about the missing boat and she agreed to meet him at Watersports in ten minutes or so.

He set off and almost immediately bumped into Superintendent Niles. They walked together briskly, both eagerly anticipating a new development in the case. They arrived and found one of the forensic technicians examining the door of Richie's Watersports cabin. It had been forced open.

'It's the speedboat,' said Richie, emerging from inside the cabin. 'Gone when I arrived at seven this morning.'

They set off for the water's edge, trying to work out a plan.

'Don't worry, they won't be getting very far,' continued Richie.

'Why?' asked the Superintendent.

'Well, I took the advice of Mr Simmons. I siphoned most of the fuel out of the motor boats a couple of days ago. Whoever they are, they're almost certainly drifting down to Oblong Island as we speak.'

The Superintendent looked at Claude and Claude shrugged. It had seemed like an obvious thing to do.

They were interrupted by the arrival of Constable

Chappell.

'It's Frank and Arlene Gough,' he puffed. 'I've searched their hut. Completely cleared out. Everyone else seems to be accounted for.'

Richie dashed off to get a jerry can of fuel and then struggled it on board the game fishing boat. He reversed the boat back up and the Superintendent, the Constable, Claude and Kath hurriedly clambered on, soaking themselves in the process. They motored slowly out through the channel.

Claude looked back as the beach began to recede from view. In the haste to get underway, he had completely forgotten about Marjorie. She appeared just as they hit the open water. Richie opened up the engines and the boat bucked and reared. There was nothing Claude could do except hang on.

Marjorie watched the boat race away and shook her head in resignation. She probably wouldn't have gone with the others anyway, but it would have been nice to have been asked. She turned away and stumped back to the hotel. She made her way to the breakfast room and sat on her own, looking as if she was trying to stir the bottom out of her coffee cup.

The problem with Marjorie was that she could become extremely unpredictable, not to say volatile, when she felt she wasn't pulling her weight. She was delighted to be part of a detective duo with someone as clever as Claude but, as far as she was concerned, the partnership only worked if she could make a contribution. And she felt that certainly hadn't been the case in the Don Anderson murder.

It was Claude who had worked out the significance of the ocean currents and Oblong Island. It was Claude who had made the difficult decision about removing the severed head from the scene. It was Claude who had taken command and instructed the manager to not only seal off the Anderson's hut but ultimately to seal off the whole island. And what had Marjorie done? She had managed to vomit all over the crime scene.

She thought back wistfully to the Stephen Kenny case. There she had managed to make a significant contribution, not least by shooting the murderer with a Glock pistol. Now, she had attempted to offer her opinion just once in the Don Anderson case and had succeeded in earning the ridicule of Superintendent Niles. Something needed to change.

She finished her breakfast and made her way to the pool. She sat down on a lounger, surveying the scene. Right in front of her was Alyssa Brown, luxuriating in the sun. She was lying on her front, loosely holding onto the sides of the lounger with each hand. She appeared to be dozing. Marjorie sat looking at her, pondering. Well, scheming.

She reached into her bag and found her phone. She fiddled with it briefly and then stood up. She walked slowly and deliberately towards Alyssa and stopped right next to her lounger. Marjorie leant forward and held up her phone. She pointed it for a second and then took a photograph.

The shutter noise caused Alyssa to stir. She turned over and sat up. Marjorie only just managed to slip her phone into the pocket of her shorts. Alyssa looked confused to find someone looming over her.

'What's happened?' she said, sleepily.

'Ah good, I was just coming over to wake you,' said Marjorie, lying profusely. 'It doesn't do to fall asleep in the sun. Very bad for that beautiful skin of yours.'

Alyssa looked even more confused. Advice on skin care from an eighty year old was a new one on her.

Marjorie smiled benignly and walked back to her lounger. She picked up her bag and set off for her hut. Once inside she shut the door and took her phone back out of her pocket again. She scrolled through her phone log and found the number she was looking for. She paused for a moment, thinking about the rules Superintendent Niles had established for her and Claude's involvement in the case: Queensland Police to be in charge at all times; the Superintendent himself to approve all investigative decisions; Claude and Marjorie only to observe and advise.

She was about to break all three of those. She dialled the number.

Meantime, Claude and the others had long since caught up with the speedboat. As predicted by Richie, the boat had run out of fuel and now dipped and bobbed idly on the swell. Oblong Island was about half a mile in the distance. Frank Gough waved his arms angrily as they approached, seemingly oblivious to any wrongdoing he might have carried out.

'Bloody boat's no good,' he shouted defiantly when Richie pulled alongside. His wife looked on, embarrassed.

Constable Chappell helped the Goughs scramble on board the game fishing boat and they found themselves immediately confronted by a stern-looking Superintendent.

'Frank and Arlene Gough, I am arresting you for stealing and taking away a motor launch from The Island Hotel.'

Arlene burst into tears. Unfortunately, that was the good part of the news.

'I am also arresting you for possible involvement in the murder of Don Anderson.'

He took a moment to read them their rights, with particular reference to their right to remain silent. Needless to say, this had the reverse effect on Frank Gough. He set off on a long tirade about his and his wife's innocence, about their illegal detention at the hotel and about their apparent victimisation by the police. Constable Chappell wrote the entire rant down in his notebook.

Kath climbed down into the speedboat with the jerry can of fuel. Claude peered over the side of the game fishing boat as she refilled the tank. He was particularly interested in the Gough's luggage which sat in the body of the boat. There were two large cases and two items of matching hand luggage, neatly stacked up. He called down to Kath and she read out the details on the luggage tags for him.

They headed back to Circular Island with Richie taking the lead and Kath following along in convoy. Arlene Gough continued to cry quietly and Frank Gough continued to berate The Queensland Police force loudly. Eventually, he ran out of steam and decided to turn his attention to Claude.

'And what are you doing here Simmons?' he asked, rudely. 'What the bloody hell does any of this have to do with you?'

Claude looked at him calmly. As ever, he didn't like

to brag about himself but the perfect riposte had popped into his head.

'Simmons? Why the formality Frank? Please, just call me Chief Superintendent.'

They arrived back at the resort and Constable Chappell led the Goughs back up the beach to one of the investigation rooms. They were watched by a sizeable crowd of guests.

This left Claude and Superintendent Niles to meander their way back together. The Superintendent was clearly interested in Claude's opinion about the Goughs and put him on the spot.

'Come on then. What do you think?'

'As you can probably tell, Frank Gough and I are hardly bosom buddies,' said Claude, as ever reluctant to give a definitive answer. 'But I remain to be convinced he's a murderer. In any case, their luggage was very odd wasn't it?'

'How do you mean?'

'Well, which self-respecting fugitives, on the run from a murder investigation, have their cases neatly packed? And their luggage tags filled out with details of their onward flight from Cairns to Brisbane?'

CHAPTER FIFTEEN

Needless to say, Frank Gough refused to be interviewed without a lawyer present. This meant that the seaplane had to be pressed into action again and the two suspects were flown back to Cairns. They were interviewed separately, each with their own lawyer present, and Superintendent Niles joined by video call. Clearly, there was little doubt about the charge of theft of the speedboat and, given the advice of his lawyer, Frank Gough admitted the offence. This may partly have been a belated attempt to protect his wife but it remained to be seen whether both would be prosecuted.

The murder charge was another matter. Both of the Goughs denied the charge vehemently and, in the case of Frank, angrily. He admitted to knowing Don Anderson and even to having had a fairly heated disagreement with him about the price of a speedboat two years before. But he and his lawyer were quick to point out that this scarcely constituted a motive for murder.

The weakness of the Goughs' defence was that they

shared an alibi. To put it plainly, they each maintained that they were in bed together at the time of the murder, fast asleep. Superintendent Niles knew that joint alibis didn't always fare well under cross examination in court and that a skilled lawyer could quickly make it seem that two guilty people were simply covering for each other. But right now, he and his colleagues were unable to find a shred of difference between the stories of the two suspects, each told in their separate interview rooms. And the real problem for the Superintendent was that he had no other means of challenging the joint alibi. The complete absence of CCTV footage from the island was a major drawback for the investigation. And nobody, staff or guest, was claiming to have seen either of the Goughs outside of their hut during the time in question.

Forensics weren't faring much better. They had completely turned the Goughs' hut upside down in the search for evidence. They examined doors, walls and floors. They scrutinised surfaces, fabrics and fibres. Even the bathroom drains were opened up and peered into. Unfortunately, the room seemed to be very much that of an ordinary holiday couple who had just checked out.

Superintendent Niles called the team together in the investigation room to share the debrief. He was beginning to look tired and careworn. He was forced to admit that, apart from their dramatic attempt to flee from the island, there was little or no evidence against the Goughs. Some forensic samples had been taken from the hut and had been sent back to the lab for analysis. Also, the Goughs' luggage was being combed through by another forensic team in Cairns. But the Superintendent didn't seem to hold out much hope.

'If the results come back negative, we'll have to release them I'm afraid. They can be bailed for the theft charge but The Crown Prosecution Service won't even think about a murder charge.'

He left the room, clearly frustrated.

Claude and Marjorie pottered around until dinner. Marjorie had specifically requested the table that was half-hidden behind the hibiscus bush and Shane led them towards it. She somehow felt that being slightly set aside from the others continued to make her and Claude's conversations look confidential and important. Or covert and surreptitious. Or something.

Shane took their orders. Claude opted for a simple main course of penne arabiata. Marjorie opted for a salad Nicoise, with the tuna steak cooked on the barbeque.

'Shall I just show the tuna the heat, Mrs Watson?'

asked Shane.

'Perfect!' said Marjorie, grinning broadly.

'What are you looking so chirpy about?' asked Claude as Shane wandered off. He was feeling almost as weighed down by the case as Superintendent Niles and couldn't understand Marjorie's perkiness.

'Me? Oh you know, ever the optimist.' She grinned again.

Claude looked at her. Ever the optimist? The last time she had started to behave like this she had ended up almost getting the pair of them thrown out of Australia.

'What are you up to Marjorie?' he asked.

She paused for a moment. 'Well, I did ring Sergeant Deacon today.'

Claude sat bolt upright in his chair.

'Why?'

'I suppose I was a bit bored. You know, when you all went off in the boat and forgot about me.'

Claude apologised. Actually, he had felt obliged to apologise twice already, what with Marjorie repeatedly referring to the incident.

'Anyway, it was nice to talk to him,' she said. 'We chatted about the case for a bit and he seemed very interested.'

'And?'

'And he told me about some nasty new virus in China that's spreading like wildfire. Apparently they've had to shut half the place down.'

Whilst this was very interesting, not to say worrying, Claude got the distinct impression that he was being side tracked. The food arrived and he decided to give up. He tucked into his pasta, suspecting that he hadn't heard half of the truth about Marjorie's day.

Indeed he hadn't.

◆ ◆ ◆

Two days later, everyone gathered at ten o'clock sharp for another debrief. Everyone except Marjorie. She had been late for breakfast that morning and had now disappeared back to her cabin, ostensibly to try and find her reading glasses. Claude set off for the meeting alone and took his seat at the back of the room.

The Superintendent's mood had not improved. The forensic testing of the Anderson's hut and their luggage had now been completed and there were no positive results. Worse still, the angry protestations by the guests and their lawyers were not only increasing but now also being directed at the Superintendent's commanding officer. This was never good news.

Everyone needed to redouble their efforts, he said.

They would begin by walking the crime scene again at midday.

The door burst open and Marjorie walked in. The Superintendent was forced to stop talking and everyone stared at her. She looked possessed.

'There's been a breakthrough. And I don't want you getting cross about it Superintendent.'

The Superintendent looked at Claude. What on earth was she talking about? Claude shrugged. He had no idea, but he strongly suspected he was about to hear the part of the story that Marjorie had so far failed to tell him.

She was brandishing a sheath of papers. She walked purposefully towards the investigation board and the Superintendent and several of the forensic technicians were forced to make way for her.

She stuck an A4 sheet of paper to the centre of the board. Clearly, Michael Hayden had been dragooned into allowing her to use the hotel's printer. The paper showed the grainy image of an engagement ring. It had been blown-up from the photo Marjorie had taken at the pool, several days earlier.

'This is Alyssa Brown's engagement ring.'

Now the Superintendent looked cross. He folded his arms. Marjorie pressed on before he had time to interrupt.

'With the help of a friend of a friend, I've been trying to find out where it was made.' She skated over the words "friend of a friend" quite quickly. 'I'm pleased to say we've tracked the ring down to a jeweller in Perth where, as I think you all know, Alyssa Brown lives.'

Everybody looked a bit confused. Where was this going?

Marjorie stepped forward and stuck a second sheet of A4 paper to the investigation board.

'And this is a credit card receipt for the purchase of that ring, six months ago.'

She stepped back to reveal a blow-up of an American Express card receipt. Everybody, including Claude, edged forward to examine it. Pandemonium broke out in the room. The credit card was in the name of "Julian D Anderson". The simple, bold signature read unmistakably as "Don Anderson".

The Superintendent walked off to the window and stared out for a moment, trying to collect his thoughts. His brain was racing. He turned back to face Marjorie. He raised his hand in attempt to restore order in the room.

'So . . . you're basically saying it's bigamy?'

'What's big of you?' asked Marjorie, slightly concerned the Superintendent was trying to take credit for her hard work.

'No, no, no Mrs Watson. Big-amy,' he said, forced to spell it out. 'You know, he was married to Lynne and he was about to about to marry Alyssa.'

'I suppose you're right. Sorry, I thought bigamy always involved long distance lorry drivers.'

Claude interrupted. 'Works perfectly well for long distance travelling salesmen.'

A clamour broke out in the room again. Everybody seemed to be speaking at once, re-examining scenarios and comparing theories. Eventually, Constable Chappell stepped forward to address the Superintendent. He was obviously worried that he and the digital team had missed a whole swathe of evidence.

'But sir, Mr Anderson never had an American Express card. He only had a Visa card and a Mastercard.'

Claude was listening to this. 'And what was the name on the Visa card and the Mastercard?'

The Constable checked briefly with the notes on the desk.

'Donald J Anderson.'

'Well there you are. If you're leading a double life you need a second set of finances. He's simply used the old trick of reversing his Christian names. I bet there'll be another bank account somewhere in the name of Julian D Anderson, to match the American Express card.'

The Superintendent thought about this. 'He'd have to feed money into it somehow so it's probably organised and funded through his company in some way,' He looked at Constable Chappell. 'Start with his secretary at CobaltBlue and . . .'

'Yes, yes, yes,' said Marjorie, slightly irritated. 'I'm sure that's all well and good. But is anyone going to arrest her?'

The Superintendent looked wide-eyed. He left the room, taking Sergeant Wilkes with him.

Claude took Marjorie off for a long walk, keen to hear the details of her investigative coup. As they set off they could see Alyssa Brown putting on her robe and being led away from the pool. All of the other guests were sat bolt upright on their loungers, eyes on stalks.

They made their way down to the water's edge and pottered along slowly.

'First of all Marjorie, bravo! How on earth did you manage it?'

The funny thing about Marjorie was that, having made a major contribution to the case, her equilibrium was now restored. She was feeling much better about herself, to the extent of even experiencing a sudden bout of modesty.

'Well you know what they say Claude. Even a blind

pig can find an acorn one day.'

Claude smiled. 'But where on earth did you get the idea?'

'Call it intuition if you like. But I didn't take to Alyssa Brown on the boat ride over. Something about her story didn't ring true. As it were.'

'And what about this friend who helped you out? Presumably that was Sergeant Deacon?'

'Oh no, it was Sergeant Mackenzie.'

'What?' Claude stopped in his tracks. Since when could Sergeant Mackenzie ever be described as Marjorie's friend? And had she lied to him about speaking to Sergeant Deacon?

Marjorie set off on a long-winded explanation. Most of her sparring with Sergeant Mackenzie had been for show, she said. Yes, he was a curmudgeon but she never thought he was stupid. She was convinced he would look back on his behaviour in the Stephen Kenny case and come to regret it. She just needed to find a way to help him take the first step.

'So I rang good old Sergeant Deacon. Got him to speak to Mackenzie and butter him up a bit. You know, offer him a chance to redeem himself. Worked a treat.'

They had now walked past Watersports and were approaching the next cove. It was beautiful and entirely deserted, apart from a group of busy sandpipers, scurrying backwards and forwards at the water's edge.

'And what about this "friend of a friend" business?' asked Claude.

"Oh yes. Well, Sergeant Mackenzie refused to do anything in an official police capacity. Fair enough. But his brother-in-law lived in Perth apparently and he happened to know someone in the jewellery trade who was prepared to ask around. So it was actually a friend of a friend of a friend. You know how it is Claude. You must have experienced that old boy network thing in the Met.'

Claude frowned, trying to work out if this was an insult or not. It probably was.

They pottered on.

'So what happens now?' asked Marjorie.

'She'll be interviewed under caution, I imagine. And we have to hope she confesses.'

'But she's as guilty as sin, isn't she? She's got to confess.'

'You'd be surprised,' said Claude.

◆ ◆ ◆

They walked to the restaurant that evening and Shane greeted them.

'Good evening,' said Marjorie. 'We'll have our usual

clandestine table please.'

They sat down behind the flowering hibiscus and Shane took them through the day's specials.

'In particular, there's a fresh catch of swordfish. We're serving it cut into thick steaks and then lightly grilled on the barbeque.'

'And is that good?' asked Marjorie.

'Oh, it's the dog's.'

This was a little confusing but, in the end, they thought they knew what he meant. Well, Marjorie was certain she knew what he meant. They decided to take his advice and Shane wandered off to speak to the chef.

He returned with their drinks and then, fifteen minutes later with their food. Served with freshly squeezed lemon and freshly ground pepper, the swordfish was indeed delicious. They finished every last morsel.

They were about to contemplate a pudding when Superintendent Niles arrived at the table. They invited him to join them and he sat down. Marjorie poured him a large glass of Claude's New Zealand pinot noir. This was an early peace offering, in case he had come to discuss Marjorie's flagrant disregard of the investigation's rules.

The Superintendent looked at Marjorie as he sipped

his wine. He was turning over in his mind Chief Constable Selby's very clear warning about her working methods.

'With regard to the "friend" you mentioned, Mrs Watson,' he said. This sounded slightly ominous. 'Are we to assume that he or she is a CHS?'

What on earth did that mean? Marjorie racked her brains. Completely Hokey Story? Cheap Hopeless Scam?

Claude intervened. He could see that the Superintendent was actually offering Marjorie a clever way out of her dilemma.

'It stands for "Confidential Human Source",' he said. 'In other words, it's an informant that only you are allowed to know about.'

Marjorie looked relieved. And pleased to now have an informant all of her own.

'In that case, yes. Strictly hush-hush, I'm afraid.'

Shane arrived to see if anyone needed anything more. Marjorie celebrated with another gin and tonic.

'I'm afraid we've still got an awful lot of work to do,' said the Superintendent as Shane disappeared.

'Have we?' asked Marjorie, naturally assuming that the case was now more or less closed.

'I'm afraid Alyssa Brown is categorically denying any involvement with the murder whatsoever.'

Claude looked at Marjorie.

The Superintendent explained that, like the Goughs, she had flatly refused to be questioned without a lawyer present. Again, this had meant her being flown back to Cairns and the Superintendent then having to carry out the interview process by video.

Her position was that she was happy to admit her relationship with Don Anderson: she had met him eighteen months before; they now shared an apartment somewhere between Perth and Fremantle; they had planned to marry in September. She had discovered the fact that he was already married six weeks before and subsequently found out about his and Lynne's planned trip to The Island Hotel. She had used the opportunity of a nearby modelling assignment to follow them there, with a view to revealing Don's double life. She was, she had said, happy to admit to intending to shame and humiliate him. But she vehemently denied having anything to do with his murder.

'She seems supremely confident,' added the Superintendent. 'She's challenged us to find any sort of DNA evidence on her clothing, in her hut or anywhere else.'

Claude thought about this for a moment. According to the pathologist, Don Anderson had been struck repeatedly on the head with something like a hammer.

And head wounds always bled profusely. If Alyssa Brown was involved in the murder, and in the subsequent manhandling of the inanimate body, then avoiding blood stains would have been almost impossible. How could she be so confident?

'Surely you're not going to let her go?' asked Marjorie, not quite believing what she was hearing and in danger of becoming outraged.

'Well, we're getting a magistrate to extend the time we've got to question her,' he said.. 'But we need to find some evidence quite soon – DNA, a weapon, anything – otherwise the Crown Prosecution service is going to start to have a problem.'

CHAPTER SIXTEEN

Another day, another debrief, this time in front of an investigation board that had a picture of Alyssa Brown as its centrepiece. They all met in the late afternoon, to allow the laboratory time to analyse all of the new material that had been collected. To no avail. The forensics team had gladly accepted Alyssa Brown's challenge and sent all of her wardrobe and most of her possessions back to Cairns for analysis. But they had been defeated. No traces of blood, no phenobarbital and nothing vaguely resembling a weapon.

Constable Chappell stood up. Alyssa Brown's electronic devices had been seized and he and the digital team in Cairns had been working on them. Initially, the information they retrieved confirmed the substance of Alyssa's story – that she and Don Anderson had met some eighteen months earlier. After that, there were merely lovey-dovey texts, emails and voice messages, exactly as you would expect from a couple in a burgeoning relationship. Significantly, one of the last emails between them came from Don, a short time before his murder, containing the lie that he was about to be away for six or seven days on a sailing trip with a major client. This had been sent from a second mobile phone that the Brisbane police had now recovered from the Anderson's house.

Apart from that, Constable Chappell had little success to report. His team's working assumption was that, just as Lynne Anderson would have needed an accomplice, then so would Alyssa Brown. Indeed, Superintendent Niles had pointed out that they couldn't rule out the possibility that Don Anderson's murder had actually been a joint enterprise between Lynne and Alyssa. After all, they both theoretically shared the same motive. However, Alyssa's electronic devices had been further examined and there were no electronic communications with any other resident on the island, including Lynne Anderson. Literally another dead end.

Claude watched from the back of the room, acutely aware of the mounting pressure on Superintendent Niles. He continued to think that Alyssa Brown was the murderer and he continued to be baffled by the complete lack of forensic evidence. He put his hand up.

'Superintendent, the hotel's laundry was shut down

after the murder. But what about the staff? Do they have a washing machine in their quarters?'

The Superintendent didn't immediately know the answer to this. He looked at Sergeant Wilkes and Constable Chappell.

'I believe they do,' said the Sergeant.

The lead forensic technician jumped to his feet, keen to defend his team's work.

'Sorry sir but even a machine wash would be very unlikely to remove all traces of blood from clothing. And we've allowed for the fact that some attempt at cleaning may have taken place. The lab has been very thorough.'

Claude thought about this. They were running out of scenarios.

'Which leaves us with two possibilities. Either she's innocent. Or she – they - have got rid of the evidence in some other way.'

'What are you thinking?' asked the Superintendent.

'Well, at times like this I try to think about what I would do.' Claude paused for a second. 'And I think I would find a remote spot on the island somewhere and then I'd have a nice big bonfire.'

The forensic team were already on their feet before Superintendent Niles had the chance to finish issuing instructions. They were joined by Sergeant Wilkes and Constable Chappell. Together they formed into two teams and set off.

Two hours later they returned, carrying a number of large bags of evidence. The search of the main body of the island had been fruitless but they had eventually found what they were looking for on the windward side of the island. There, on a small rocky cove, probably not much used by guests, were the ashes of a large driftwood bonfire.

Marjorie looked at the clear plastic bags as the forensic technicians headed towards the seaplane. They appeared to be full of nothing more than black ash.

'Are they going to be able to find anything amongst that lot?' she asked Claude.

Claude looked at the bags. He didn't think it seemed likely either.

'I think you may have noticed on this trip that modern forensic science has rather left me behind,' he said, modestly. 'But I'm hoping it might at least buy the Superintendent some time with the magistrate. You know, while the lab analyses it. It might just keep the baying mob at arms length for another day.'

◆ ◆ ◆

On the following morning there was still no news. Claude and Marjorie enjoyed a leisurely lunch and then made their way to the pool. They were about to choose a pair of loungers when they became aware of a disturbance coming from somewhere on the beach. They followed the noise and realised it was actually a group of people shouting, some of them quite angrily. It was coming from Watersports and when they arrived, the cause of the commotion became obvious. The baby turtles were hatching out.

Word had obviously gone round quickly and there was already a crowd of about twenty guests. But it was anything but an uplifting experience. A crowd of raucous seagulls had also arrived. Unfortunately, they weren't regarding the baby turtles as a joyous example of nature's miracles. They were regarding them as lunch. Claude and Marjorie watched as one baby turtle wobbled and tottered its way down towards the sea. It had almost made it when a seagull swooped down and picked it up cleanly in its beak. The seagull wheeled away in triumph.

'No!' shouted Marjorie loudly, joining in with the angry clamour from the other guests. For the time being, everybody had forgotten about the murder of Don Anderson and become obsessed with the murder of the turtles.

Luckily, Richie arrived at the scene. He had seen this sort of thing happen before and he had a solution. He sprinted back to the rear of the Watersports cabin and returned with a huge armful of palm fronds, cut down recently by the gardeners. He handed out the fronds and then formed the guests into two lines, one either side of the path the turtles were taking down to the sea. It looked like some sort of strangely improvised Guard of Honour. But it worked.

Two more babies emerged from the nest and started to meander their way towards the sea. The guests waved their palm fronds aggressively at the seagulls and shouted at them at the tops of their voices. The gulls hovered and flapped and screeched and squawked. Several tried gamely to break through the whirling canopy. But each time they were forced to retreat. After what seemed an age but what was probably only a minute, the turtles made it to the water. They were immediately collected by a wave and, after some brief experimental paddling, disappeared off into the ocean.

The guests clapped and cheered and hugged each other. It felt as if, in the intensity of the moment, they were engaged in saving the planet itself.

Not that their work was done. The baby turtles simply kept coming and everybody continued to wave and scream and, in the case of Marjorie, swear at the gulls. When anyone became tired there were willing replacements from the additional crowd of guests that had arrived. They suffered one more tragic loss but eventually the final baby turtle made its way into the sea.

The guests slowly began to disappear, some of them arm in arm. Claude and Marjorie hung back to congratulate Richie on the success of the rescue mission.

'Thanks,' he said, 'it's the same every year. A green turtle lays over one hundred eggs so the game is trying to keep as many of the babies alive as possible. I think we did pretty well this year.'

'So you'll be letting the university in Sydney know, presumably?' asked Claude.

'Yeah, they'll be pleased. Every single baby's been recorded so they'll be getting the data tomorrow.'

Claude and Marjorie let Richie get on with clearing up after the battle and they wandered back along the beach towards the hotel. They were each lost in their thoughts for a moment until Claude suddenly stopped. He turned round and stood staring back at Watersports, as if he was trying to work something out.

'What did he mean by "recorded"?' he asked.

'What did he mean by what?' asked Marjorie.

'Richie said all the baby turtles had been "recorded". What did he mean? Did you see him or anyone else with a notebook?'

'I'm afraid I didn't.' Marjorie had been far too busy swearing at gulls to really notice anything at all.

Claude thought about this for a moment longer. Then he set off back towards Watersports as fast as he could go.

'Come on, there's no time to waste,' he said, urgently.

Marjorie followed behind, struggling to catch up yet again.

They found Richie picking up the last of the palm fronds. Claude launched straight in.

'Were you counting all the turtles as they emerged?'

Richie looked surprised. This was a sudden and unexpected question. He shook his head.

'No. There was no need.'

'Why not?'

'Well, the whole thing was recorded by the webcam.'

'Webcam? What webcam?'

Richie pointed back to the Watersports cabin. Just below the roof, a small camera had been attached. You would never have noticed it if you didn't know it was there.

'But the hotel has no CCTV,' said Marjorie, struggling to follow. 'It's company policy.'

Richie shrugged, still not understanding what all

the fuss was about. 'It's got nothing to do with the hotel. It belongs to the Marine Institute and they came up and installed it themselves.'

'Good grief!' said Claude, clasping his hand to his forehead. 'Can we see some of the footage please?'

Richie led them back to the cabin. He explained that the webcam was linked to his desktop computer. He ordinarily collected the data one month at a time and then sent it back to Sydney for them to analyse it. He sat down at his desk and tapped away at the keyboard. After a few seconds, images of the escaping turtles appeared.

Claude leant forward and peered at the screen. There in the middle of the picture was the turtle's nest, with the babies burrowing their way out from the sand. And there were the two lines of guests, waving their palm fronds and shouting at the tops of their voices. But he was more interested in something else. There, in the extreme right of the frame, was the collection of kayaks and canoes, neatly pulled up on the beach.

Claude stood back up and looked at Richie. 'Is this set to permanently record? Even at night?'

'Yeah, but . . .'

Richie looked at the screen and then back at Claude. He had suddenly realised what all the fuss was about.

He set about lining up the footage. Claude picked up the phone. He dialled reception and asked to be put through to Superintendent Niles.

'Superintendent,' he said as the phone was answered. 'You're needed down at Watersports. I think we might have something important to show you.'

Five minutes later, everyone was stood behind Richie's computer screen, with the Superintendent still trying to process all the information he'd just been given about webcams, turtles and The Marine Institute in Sydney. Richie had found the footage for the night of the murder and had paused at midnight. With everyone ready he set the film in motion, adjusting the settings so that it ran at four times normal speed. For a long time nothing happened and they were left staring anxiously at the turtle's nest and the sign that read, "Sshh, turtle eggs!".

Then, just after 3 am, there was a sudden burst of activity. Richie stopped the film and went back. He set it running again at normal speed and everyone leant forward for a better view. Suddenly a man appeared, dragging a body slowly towards the canoes and kayaks. He let the body fall to the floor and stood up.

'Who is it?' asked the Superintendent.

Richie paused the frame and peered intently at the black and white image.

'Bloody hell!' He sat back in his chair. 'It's Barry Grogan!'

Marjorie looked at Claude. Barry the cocktail designer had now graduated to Barry the murderer.

Richie set the footage running again. After several seconds, Alyssa Brown entered the frame. She appeared to be using her foot to kick sand over the traces left by Don Anderson's body being dragged along. Everybody watched intently as Barry untied one of the canoes and dragged it half into the water. Then he lifted the body again and this time Alyssa stepped forward to help. She picked up Don Anderson's legs and together, after something of a struggle, they manhandled him into the back seat of the canoe. Barry pushed the boat back into the water and then jumped in himself. He paddled away with Don Anderson slumped behind him, one arm dangling in the water. He disappeared from frame.

Ten minutes later he paddled back in, this time alone in the canoe. He jumped out and began splashing sea water over the boat, presumably trying to wash off traces of blood. Alyssa arrived to help but they didn't seem very happy with the results. Barry took off his polo shirt soaked it in the sea and began rubbing the boat vigorously.

The Superintendent had seen enough. He stood up,

breathing an audible sigh of relief.

'Thank you all,' he said. He shook Claude and Marjorie by the hand. 'And Mr Gilmour, I'm afraid you're going to need a new computer. Someone will be along to take this one away in a minute.'

He turned and left.

◆ ◆ ◆

The next day, Claude and Marjorie took a farewell stroll along the beach with Superintendent Niles. Fundamentally, the case was solved and, apparently, the Crown Prosecution Service was now happy to charge Alyssa Brown and Barry Grogan with murder.

The guests were free to leave, including Lynne Anderson. Even the Goughs were in the clear, with the hotel deciding not to press charges for the theft of the boat. The Superintendent himself was flying back to Cairns with the remainder of his team later that afternoon.

Marjorie had spent the morning booking hers and Claude's flights home. They were planning to leave the next day, stopping a couple of extra nights in Sydney along the way.

'Since you're heading home, am I to assume you've finally found the weapon?' asked Claude.

The Superintendent looked at them both, laughing.

'Yes, and it means I've finally been able to make a contribution to the case,' he said, mocking himself slightly again. 'I treated the team to a cocktail at the pool bar, as a thank you for all their hard work. And there was the weapon, hiding in plain sight.'

'What? Where?' asked Marjorie.

'Taking pride of place amongst all of the assorted cocktail making paraphernalia. It was Barry Grogan's chromium plated ice hammer.'

'No!' Marjorie looked horrified.

'I'm afraid so. The pathologist has confirmed it fits Don Anderson's wounds perfectly.'

'But Barry was using that to make all my drinks. Yuk!'

They walked on, scattering a small group of sandpipers.

'And the phenobarbital?' asked Claude.

'We never found another trace of it. Neither Ms Brown or Mr Grogan are being particularly cooperative at the moment but they will in the end. For the moment we're assuming whatever they had left went into the ocean with the body. There may be a drugged-up tiger shark swimming around very slowly somewhere.'

'But the theory is that Barry Grogan had slipped most of it into the Andersons' late night coffees?'

'Absolutely.'

It was Marjorie's turn.

'The thing I can't fathom is how much of a spell Alyssa Brown cast over Barry in such a short space of time.'

The Superintendent thought about this.

'We've checked both of their call logs and their emails. It looks as if they'd never met before she arrived on the island. So you're right, he's gone from happy-go-lucky barman to murderer in about four days flat.'

Marjorie frowned.

'Well that's what I definitely call a rush of blood. Although not necessarily to the head.'

CHAPTER SEVENTEEN

Claude and Marjorie had said their fond farewells to Shane and the rest of the hotel's staff. Now they had made their way to reception and were greeted by Michael Hayden. If they had enjoyed something of a victory lap after their success at the Farm Hotel, they were about to be afforded a lap of honour on their trip to Sydney.

It began with Mr Hayden heaping praise on them. The suggestion that they might both have been some sort of bad luck charm seemed to have long since been forgotten and they were now acknowledged as conquering heroes. He explained that the Elysium Leisure Group, owners of both The Island Hotel and The Farm, wanted to particularly express their gratitude to Claude and Marjorie for now solving the second murder. Evidently, most of Australia had been following the Anderson case on television and in the newspapers, thanks largely to camera phone footage happily provided by the disgruntled guests. This meant that the hotel had never received so much publicity and, in spite of the rather macabre context, they were now booked out for the next twelve weeks straight.

'That's our pleasure Mr Hayden,' said Marjorie. 'Being trapped here with a juicy murder thrown in was extremely diverting.'

The manager frowned slightly. He was hoping for a compliment from Marjorie in return. He wasn't entirely sure he'd received it.

Claude picked up his hand luggage.

'Right then Marjorie, we've got a boat to catch.'

'Forgive me,' said Michael Hayden, 'but I don't think so.'

He gestured to the open door and the beach and the ocean beyond. Tethered to a buoy outside the reef was the seaplane.

'All yours,' he said, smiling. 'Compliments of Superintendent Niles and the Queensland Police.'

They wandered down to the beach and found Richie and the speedboat waiting for them. They motored out slowly and tied up next to the seaplane. The luggage was loaded on and they prepared to board. Claude shook Richie warmly by the hand. Marjorie stepped forward and gave him a big hug.

'If I were sixty years younger,' she said, rather ridiculously. Richie gave a big Australian grin in return.

Marjorie stopped at the door of the plane and looked

back at the island. Notwithstanding her slightly lukewarm comment to Michael Hayden, she was definitely going to miss it. A small number of the original guests remained and they had gathered on the beach to watch Claude and Marjorie leave. Marjorie gave them one of her waves and clambered into the plane.

They set off with Marjorie humming the Indiana Jones theme tune. The plane circled the island once and headed for Cairns, flying low over the vast area of reef and tropical islands. They gazed out of the window, soaking up their last glimpse of the myriad blues of the beautiful Coral Sea.

They transferred to the main airport in Cairns and boarded their plane for Sydney. This leg of their journey would take about two hours and fifty minutes and was what Marjorie, now a seasoned Australian traveller, was referring to as a "short-hop" flight. In Sydney, she had booked them into the same hotel on the water front at The Rocks. They settled themselves in, changed for dinner and eventually made their way to the Hotel's restaurant. Claude felt the least he could do was order the curried blue-eyed cod again and this time afford the chef the service of actually eating it. It was superb.

The next day, they opted for some blatant, unabashed sightseeing. In the morning, the hotel had organised them a two hour tour of the city by boat. They sat back and enjoyed the close-up views of the landmarks, the bays, and the famous beaches. Unfortunately for Claude, Marjorie couldn't resist one last running commentary about the straightforwardness of Aussie names: Circular Quay because it was a quay shaped liked a circle; Sydney Harbour Bridge because it was a bridge in Sydney Harbour; Manly Beach because it was a beach full of manly surfers (actually, she made this last one up). In the afternoon they walked to the Royal Botanical Gardens and then took the guided tour of the magnificent Sydney Opera House. They arrived back at the hotel in time for a refreshing snooze before dinner.

They had booked a table for the evening at a Chinese restaurant, situated in a huge old warehouse at the water's edge. Claude arrived at the hotel's reception first and was greeted by several members of staff who, for some reason, were beaming at him. He was followed shortly by Marjorie who swept in wearing her finest outfit and a not inconsiderable amount of make-up. He really should have known that something was amiss.

The manager stepped forward to open the door for them as they left. They stepped out into the street, to be greeted by a throng of paparazzi. They found themselves immediately in the middle of a barrage of cameras, flashlights and incessant questions. Claude was completely taken aback but Marjorie seemed to be thoroughly enjoying herself. Strangely, she seemed to be smiling and waving in the direction of one particular photographer.

Eventually, Claude prised her free from the scrum and they set off to walk to the restaurant.

'I had no idea that was going to happen, did you?' he asked, still slightly shocked.

'Well . . .' said Marjorie.

Claude stopped in his tracks and looked at her.

'I've been keeping in touch with that nice Ellie Hartmann from The Alice Advertiser,' she went on. 'Didn't you see me waving to her just then?'

'And what did you tell her?'

'Just that we were coming to Sydney. Where's the harm in that? I've no idea how all those other people found out.'

Claude wasn't sure whether Marjorie was being wilfully naïve or wilfully misleading. He felt he didn't have the energy to investigate one way or the other.

The restaurant was large but nonetheless crowded and bustling. In the centre was a large round table which, judging by the attentions of the waiting staff, seemed to be full of VIPs. Claude and Marjorie were ushered to a quieter table, overlooking the harbour. They sat studying their menus, almost overwhelmed by the incredible amount of choice. In the end, they opted to share everything and simply chose their favourites: salt and pepper squid; prawn sesame toast; pot sticker dumplings; half a crispy duck with pancakes and plum sauce.

They were halfway through their meal when they became aware of someone walking purposefully towards them. He wore a smart suit and seemed to have come from the VIP table. He stopped in front of them and Claude and Marjorie realised that everyone on the surrounding tables had gone quiet.

'Look, I just wanted to come over and say thank you for everything you've done,' he said. 'It's a fantastic thing you've achieved and you've had the whole of Australia on the edge of its seat. I think I speak for everyone when I say we'd love to have you back sometime soon.'

Misunderstanding slightly, Marjorie opened her handbag and pulled out one of her business cards. She handed it to him.

'That's very kind of you. And here's my telephone number, should the situation arise.' She was never one to miss out on what she thought was a new business opportunity. 'We're always happy to discuss your murder needs, big or small.'

He looked at the card, entirely nonplussed. Out of politeness he put it in his pocket. He thanked them both again and wandered back to his table, gently shaking his head.

Claude turned to the woman on the next table.

'Sorry, who was that?'

'Oh, that would be the Prime Minister.'

◆ ◆ ◆

They made their way to Sydney's Kingsford Smith airport the next morning. Marjorie had booked them two business class seats but as they approached the check-in desk they were intercepted by one of the Qantas ground crew.

'Mrs Watson, Mr Simmons, would you mind coming with me please?'

Marjorie was immediately nervous. She had bought two bottles of gin in Sydney and wasn't at all sure what the regulations were and, for that matter, whether the airline or the airport were in charge of strip searches. She needn't have worried. They were led a short distance to the first class desk where another ground crew member greeted them with a smile. They had been upgraded.

Ten minutes later they were sat in the enormous

first class lounge, marvelling at their continuing good fortune. Marjorie signed into the wifi and typed a google search into her iPad. The result came up immediately.

'Ha!' she said, studying the screen. She passed the iPad to Claude. It showed the front page of the Alice Advertiser, featuring an article by Ellie Hartmann. The headline read, rather imaginatively:

"Dodo Detectives Conquer Queensland!"

Underneath was a large photograph of Claude and Marjorie boarding the seaplane, obviously taken yet again with a guest's camera phone. Marjorie was waving regally and looked, for all the world, as if she was about to begin the second or third leg of a Commonwealth Tour.

Claude got up and walked to the newspaper rack. He studied the selection on offer and eventually returned with a copy of the Guardian for himself and three Australian papers for Marjorie.

'More for your scrapbook,' he said, handing them to her.

She was delighted. Each one featured a front page article about their antics. One had a photograph of them taken outside the hotel, with Marjorie waving as if she was on the red carpet. The other two had photos of them being thanked by the Prime Minister, presumably taken by fellow diners. The headlines all seemed to be following Ellie Hartmann's lead and competing for the most imaginative nickname for the detective duo.

The most sober of the newspapers had gone with:

"Senior Sleuths Take Australia By Storm"

A second paper described Claude and Marjorie as "The Decrepit Detectives". A third, an unpleasant tabloid, had opted for "The Incontinent Investigators".

Claude read the papers over her shoulder.

'I think it's lucky we're leaving now. We could be the putrid pensioners by the end of the week.'

Marjorie, who always cleaved to the principle that any publicity was good publicity, was delighted with it all. She folded the three newspapers neatly and tucked them into her hand luggage.

'Anyway, that's enough of all that,' she said, sitting up straight and abruptly changing the subject. 'Now what about that two dollars you owe me, Claude?'

Claude put down his Guardian, seemingly taken aback.

'No, no, no, Marjorie. I think you'll find that we're quits.'

'How can we possibly be quits?'

'But that was point of the double or nothing bet you accepted at The Island Hotel. I offered you a chance to get your money back. You were therefore agreeing that you'd lost the initial bet.'

She looked at him.

'Oh that's what double or nothing means. I did wonder.'

She paused for a moment.

'But I didn't lose the first bet. So by your own logic you owe me two dollars.'

A member of staff arrived to let them know it was time to board the plane. They both got up, Claude somewhat wearily. They picked up their hand luggage and set off, arguing the merits of the Stephen Kenny case yet again. They boarded the plane and made their way to the first class cabin, still bickering. They hadn't stopped by the time the pilot had taxied to the end of the runway. Claude was desperately trying to distinguish between random and coincidence for the umpteenth time. He ended by pointing out that the two words weren't even synonyms for each other, thinking that this somehow clinched the argument. He didn't seem to realise that he'd perhaps got a little lost in his own detail.

Marjorie had been listening intently.

'I've got two things to say about all that, Claude.'

The plane began to race down the runway. She had to shout to be heard above the roar of the engines.

'Firstly, you'll be pleased to know I'm reverting to English slang now that we're flying home. And secondly, what a load of old cobblers.'

BOOKS IN THIS SERIES

The Dilapidated Detectives

The Dilapidated Detectives

The Dilapidated Detectives Down Under

Printed in Great Britain
by Amazon